P9-EMP-151

DISCARD

One Amazing Elephant

One Amazing Elephant

Linda Oatman High

HARPER

An Imprint of HarperCollins*Publishers*

One Amazing Elephant

Copyright © 2017 by Linda Oatman High

All rights reserved. Printed in the United States of America.

No part of this book may be used or reproduced in any manner whatsoever without written permission except in the case of brief quotations embodied in critical articles and reviews. For information address HarperCollins Children's Books, a division of HarperCollins Publishers, 195 Broadway, New York, NY 10007.

www.harpercollinschildrens.com

Library of Congress Control Number: 2016935896
ISBN 978-0-06-245583-3

Typography by Erin Fitzsimmons
17 18 19 20 21   CG/LSCH   10 9 8 7 6 5 4 3 2 1

❖

First Edition

R0447722930

In memory of my father, Robert L. Haas.
I had three elephants on my bedroom wall
and plenty of books on my shelves.
Thank you, Dad.

Riding the Elephant

I'm finally riding the elephant, my grandpa Bill's circus elephant, Queenie Grace, and it feels kind of like I'm riding the universe. I'm perched on top of this unsteady world (a nervous pachyderm cowgirl), sitting way high up on a slow-rolling wrinkly gray world of elephant. And the elephant is related to me. The elephant is like a child to Grandpa Bill and Grandma Violet; they've had her for thirty years. Much longer than I've been alive.

I wheeze. I do this when I'm stressed, especially in the heat. I sweat. My legs itch with red welts from mosquito bites. Riding an elephant isn't as exotic or special as it looks on websites about jungles. Some people even have it on their bucket lists: "Ride an elephant!" Well, I don't have a bucket list, but even if I did, this would not be on it. I'm doing it for my grandpa.

"Way to go, Lily!" cheers Grandpa Bill, pride rising in his scratchy voice as he hobbles alongside his elephant. "I always did say that you'd make up your mind and finally ride Queenie Grace one day! Conquer that fear and be brave! Yay!"

Grandpa's smile stretches like a rubber band across his face.

I just nod, eyes fixed straight ahead, because there are times in life that a person can't say a word.

My legs clench loose folds of sun-scorched elephant skin; so do my hands. I grit my teeth, set my jaw, make my arms stiff and strong. I will not let go, not until I'm getting safely off this huge animal. The grass—plus good solid earth and dirt—is looking awfully good right about now. I don't belong in the sky. I don't belong this high.

"It's okay, Lily," Grandpa Bill says with a grin, looking up at me with those kind blue eyes. "Queenie Grace is very careful. She'd never hurt you."

That's easy for him to say: My grandfather—the Giant—has been the elephant's best friend forever.

Grandpa Bill is called the Giant because he is seven feet five inches tall. He works in the circus, advertised as "The Amazing Queenie Grace and her Best Friend, Bill the Giant!" and so does my small grandma Violet, who is just four feet nine inches. And then there's Queenie Grace, who's nine feet three inches. It feels much higher when you're sitting on top of that rolling universe of elephant, holding on for dear life.

But I've just turned twelve, so it's about time that I finally ride the elephant. That's what they've all been telling me, anyway.

Grandpa Bill continues to shuffle along by my side, one brown-spotted hand on the elephant. It's so hot, smack-dab in the middle of summertime, and the pesky burn of the sun rests heavy on my head. Grandpa Bill stumbles a little but catches himself. He has super-big feet, and every now and then he gets a bit clumsy.

My grandparents are here in West Virginia because their circus—Haas-Millard Brothers—has a show near my home. And so they are visiting, along with my long-lost mother, Trullia Lee Pruitt, the Girl on the Flying Trapeze.

My mother's side of the family comes from a long line— a long quivery *wire*—of circus people. Tightrope walkers, high-flying trapeze artists, tiger tamers, elephant trainers. And my mom, well, truth is she ran off to rejoin that circus she grew up with. She hit the road in a glittery gold trapeze girl outfit, and apparently, she never looked back.

"You're doing a great job, Lily!" Grandpa Bill says as Queenie Grace trudges along in the yard near my home at the campground. Her big feet kick up dust, as it hasn't rained in a while. I sneeze and wheeze. It's pollen season: all the flowers and trees are bursting with blooms. Bees buzz lazily around us. I feel the elephant's skin flinch when they fly near.

"I have this feeling that before too long, you and Queenie Grace will be great friends," says Grandpa Bill.

I look down at the top of my grandpa's head, where there's a little circle of worn baldness, a patch of pinkish-red head that I can see from up here. I know my grandfather's face by heart, but this bald space is something I've never seen before today.

"I . . . don't know," I say. "I really can't imagine me and an elephant actually being *friends*. But being up here, at least that's a big step."

I feel like I can see for miles, all of Magic Mountain Campground, with its blue-bottomed swimming pool and pirate-themed mini-golf course. It's busy this time of the year.

"Well, you might be surprised," Grandpa Bill says. "Life can throw some big curveballs, and I don't know why, but I have this feeling about you two. . . ."

He's just saying that. Grandpa Bill has tried all kinds of tricks through the years, to try to get me to really love his elephant. To push past my stupid fear.

Grandpa gives Queenie Grace the little clicking sound with his mouth that means *Stop now*. She listens, coming to a standstill, skin still swaying. Her ears flap; her tail swishes. She snuffles. I wonder if carrying me feels like hard work to her.

Grandpa reaches into the pocket of his shorts, pulls out a carrot.

"She deserves a treat," Grandpa Bill says. "She's such a good girl."

I'm trying hard to believe that, especially now that my life depends on that fact. I think maybe I'm getting just a little bit brave.

The elephant inhales the carrot, the universe of her big body still rolling and shifting beneath me.

Then Grandpa leads the way, quietly whistling his favorite tune that he says always makes Queenie Grace follow: "Amazing Grace."

Grandpa walks around and around our yard at Magic Mountain, the elephant right behind him like an obedient kid. I'm sorry that the others are inside and not out here watching, because this is a "Step Right Up" kind of moment for Lily Rose Pruitt.

Step right up! See the girl who has just turned twelve finally get up the courage to ride the elephant!

Queenie Grace Is Good at Taking Care of People

I am so happy! I am finally giving a ride to the frightened girl, Bill's granddaughter, Lily.

I like the weight of the child on my back. I enjoy feeling strong and helpful, walking along carefully so as not to fall. I will take care of her, for my best friend, Bill. I am very good at taking care of people.

I was twenty-eight when I came to my nice people, sweet Bill the Giant and his tiny wife, Violet. They are kind. Both have gentle eyes. I do like my life these days. And now I am fifty-eight!

Bill is my trainer, my caretaker, my *mahout*. He saved me, rescued me from people who did not know how to treat an elephant. I adore my *mahout*.

I work in the circus, at fairs, sometimes at schools. We

are called "The Amazing Queenie Grace and Her Best Friend, Bill the Giant!" We travel. I do tricks, like picking up someone to carry, folded soft and warm as a towel inside my trunk, or kneeling to say a prayer. I paint. I hold the brush carefully. The people cheer and clap. They buy my paintings.

My keeper Bill taught me to paint. He taught me to paint and to pray and to pick someone up so gently in my trunk. Bill has taught me many things, and I like to think I have taught him things, too.

Like now: I am teaching Bill the Giant how to make his granddaughter be brave. I am being so careful with the girl Lily Rose Pruitt.

And she might be starting to like me, maybe just a teeny bit. *I wonder if we will ever be friends.*

"Good girl," Lily whispers. She pats my skin, gingerly, lightly. "Good girl. Don't let me fall, okay?"

I will not let her fall. I would never let her fall.

In the Spotlight

Grandpa Bill helps me down, making a step with his hands by intertwining his fingers together.

"Grab my neck, Lily," he says. "I won't let you fall."

And I know he won't. I circle his wrinkled old neck with both arms, holding on as Grandpa slowly lowers me to the ground.

"Whew," I say. "That was . . . crazy!"

"Fun, right?"

"Um, I don't know about *fun*, exactly. But at least I faced my fear, and gave it a try."

"So, Lily, I have an idea," says Grandpa Bill. "How about you star in the circus tonight? Kick off the first show of the evening by riding into the big top on Queenie Grace! The audience loves when an elephant starts the show."

"That's usually Grandma's job," I say.

"I'm sure she wouldn't mind sharing the spotlight," Grandpa says.

I look at the ground, toe the grass with my sneaker.

"Um . . . I don't know, Grandpa. I'm kind of shy."

"I know," Grandpa Bill says. "But there's no need to be. You're a star, Lily! Show the world! Let your light shine!"

I shrug.

"I don't know . . ."

He smiles, and like always, Grandpa Bill melts my heart like caramel in the sun.

"Okay," I say. "I'll do it, Grandpa. I'll do it for you."

Riding the elephant into the red-and-white-striped tent, filled with neighbors and friends and kids from school, I am jittery but proud. Wearing a shimmery pink shirt that Grandma Violet found for me, with my wild red hair tamed into a ponytail, I feel important. Special. Even pretty.

I see Dad's face. He lights up, waves like crazy when he sees me. You'd think the sun rises and sets on Lily Rose Pruitt, the way my dad acts.

My mother, Trullia, must be in one of the trailers, getting all dressed up for her trapeze act, which involves lots of makeup, hair straightening with a hot iron, and a tight, glittery leotard.

Or maybe Trullia's hanging out in the row of silver-submarine

1960s Airstream trailers that house interesting people like the bearded lady and the conjoined twins and the three men with small heads. Some people might call them "freaks," but to me they're just Mary and Harry and Larry and Wilmer and Herbert and Walt. Not a lot of circuses still have "freak shows" these days, but the Haas-Millard circus does. The "freaks" are a big attraction for this little circus. Sometimes I wonder if I'll be a "freak," too, on account of already being over five feet seven inches tall, and being related to the Giant. It might run in the family.

Grandpa Bill limps ahead of me and the elephant, hoisting a flag. The happy circus music starts; Queenie Grace plods into the tent. It's warm in here and smells like roasted peanuts and buttery popcorn. The audience cheers and claps along to the tune. I wave like Grandpa taught me, smile like I'm not nervous, hold on tight. At least this time, there's a saddle to keep me in place.

A sea of faces swims before me.

Like usual, my mother is nowhere in sight.

The story of my mother goes like this: I was three years old when she took off. She left me and Dad in her dust at Magic Mountain Campground, where we get to live rent-free in exchange for my dad being the maintenance guy. He keeps everything going, and I do mean *everything*.

And so she was gone, off to the circus she always loved.

It's been just Dad and me ever since.

Don't get me wrong. I love my dad. I love West Virginia. I love Magic Mountain Campground and I love our cozy little cabin.

But what I don't exactly love is that she could actually run away from her daughter. I don't love that I get to see her face maybe once a year, if that, whenever the circus happens to be playing nearby.

And what I certainly don't love is that she wasn't watching me the day that Queenie Grace almost killed me.

Once upon a time, I almost died.

This is what I remember: gray, a high stretch of gray like an alive and stormy day. Acres of gray wrinkled skin, an entire crumpled *landscape* of elephant.

It smelled like a whole world full of wild. The dangerous eyes, a fierce shiny dark. The swishing tail, flappy ears, bristly rough hairs, the snuffling sounds of its breath, the swinging trunk.

I was six, with a bad case of asthma. I didn't just breathe; I wheezed. Same as now.

My grandparents were visiting from Florida on account of a nearby gig, and my long-lost mom was along, too.

My grandparents' rickety old motor home was parked in our yard, with the big hitch hooked up to the elephant trailer. (The trailer was painted in rainbow colors and excitement:

The Amazing Queenie Grace and Her Best Friend, Bill the Giant!)

The elephant roamed free that day, its trunk sucking something from a huge bucket. My grandparents chatted in the cabin with my dad, and my mother was supposed to be watching me, except she was really drifting away like the smoke from her cigarette.

I was riding my brand-new pink bike with the bell, the white wicker basket, and the shiny silver spokes.

"Mommy!" I called. "Look at me! Watch!"

I was so proud that I could ride alone, no training wheels, no help.

"Mommy!" I called again. I rang the bell. I remember that I swerved so I wouldn't run over a ladybug.

And then I fell. The bike tipped. Slivers of stones stuck sharp in my bony knees. I was bleeding. I began screaming, and this is the part where I really started to maybe not trust Trullia Pruitt.

Miss Trullia Lee Pruitt just kept on smoking. The tip of her cigarette glowed red against a sunset sky. Her frizzy hair made a silhouette, just a fuzzy dark outline of a mother, and her eyes floated far away in the sky.

"Help me!" I screamed. It was summer, dust dry in my mouth. My knees burned, my belly churned from the sight of blood. One of the bicycle pedals was still moving, round and round, spinning.

My mother did not answer. She did not move. But the elephant did.

The animal's gray skin rippled and rolled, and it lumbered fast across the yard. Then it slowly lay down on the ground, arranged all that skin right beside me, so close I could feel its hot air on my face.

I held my breath, pulled my stinging knees tight to my chest. Curled up like a comma, everything paused. I could feel the weight, the heat. I could smell elephant, and it pushed even closer to my side. I thought I was going to die. I could not breathe right. My knees were bleeding, and my own mother was doing nothing.

Luckily for me, Grandpa Bill came into view, towering tall and thin, his head looming.

"Queenie Grace, roll away," he said, in a quiet, calm voice.

And the elephant did. It rolled sluggishly and then it stood, flinging its trunk, snorting.

"Good girl," crooned my grandpa. He patted the elephant's back.

And then Grandpa Bill lifted me, pressing his clean white handkerchief lightly to each of my bleeding knees. Red bled through, blotches like flowers.

"Oh, Lily girl," he said. "I'll fix this."

My grandfather held me close, my head pressed next to his heart, and he carried me inside.

Grandpa washed me up and got me some ice-cold

lemonade, and he found some Minnie Mouse Band-Aids in the medicine cabinet. He covered my cuts and he cuddled me in the rocking chair. Grandpa Bill's love was like a glove: fuzzy and snug and warm and soft. Grandma Violet kept stroking my head, and Dad kissed each knee.

But Trullia? All she did was cough. My mother coughed and coughed, a deep empty rattle where her heart should have been, and then she just strolled off the porch to smoke another cigarette.

She apparently didn't have fear, didn't even seem to be one bit afraid of her little girl being hurt.

I stayed far away from the elephant from that day on, and I think that's when I started to be so scared of her. Grandpa tried so hard, every summer when I saw him, to push me past the fear, to make me brave, but it never worked. I stayed afraid . . . until today, anyway. Now, maybe I am brave.

"You need to forgive, Lily," Dad always tells me. "Only when people forgive do they truly begin to live. You need to get over it, sweetheart."

But that's easy for him to say. My dad's not a twelve-year-old girl whose mother ran off and joined the circus. I know it's been hard for him, too, but at least he's not a kid. Plus, he knew that Trullia was a circus girl from the moment they met.

And so I'm thinking about all this as I ride into the spotlight when all of a sudden the elephant breaks into a run.

She bolts, thundering all the way across the tent, as I hold on for dear life.

The audience obviously thinks this is part of the show, and they applaud and cheer.

But they don't know what I know from way up here: I have it again. The fear. The fear is back, and it's worse than ever.

Queenie Grace Meant No Harm

I meant no harm. I never meant to frighten that odd girl Lily, not when she was little and not tonight, when the bee scared me.

When Lily was tiny, I was protecting her! I also saved the girl's mother one time. I saved Trullia's life. I kept her from hurting herself that one night when her illness was very bad. I grabbed the knife in my trunk, carefully, so carefully, and I took it away from Trullia.

And so I knew that I could save the girl Lily, too.

I still remember that day in West Virginia, when Lily was very young. Trullia was smoking. Blowing. In. Out. In. Out.

I saw the child. She wobbled, riding the bike. I saw her fall. And I heard her screams.

I tried to comfort her, lying by her side. I tried to calm

the crying child. I did not want her to be afraid, to be alone, to be hurt.

Oh, I know about hurt. I know about blood. I know of fear and I know about tears. I know loneliness and I know pain, and I certainly know how it is to be afraid.

My first owner, in a faraway country, before here, before Bill, kept me in chains. He beat me. He made me bleed. I had red raw scrapes on my knees, on my legs. I ached from the switch, my skin worn thin. That man, that first owner, shot my parents when I was little. I always wished somebody would come and save me.

I learned in that other country how to be fearful of people. I learned to feel hate.

Then I came to the United States, on a ship. My spirit and my skin broken, sick.

I was sold to angry men who reeked of greed, circus workers. I lived for more than two years with eight other elephants, all of us treated the same. We were a family, though. When I became heavy and tired with pregnancy, I realized I was going to have a child. I felt the baby move within, shifting, kicking. Feeling that life kept me alive. Twenty-two months I carried my child inside.

But then the men took the baby away, soon after it came into the world. Those men made me feel hate once again, stronger than ever. They took my baby, my Little Gray.

She looked back at me, that day she was taken. I was chained. I pulled and pulled! I could not break the chains. I could not save my baby.

To this day, I think of her with great pain. I wish they had allowed her to stay. I pray. I know how to go down on my knees. I raise my eyes to the sky and I cry out on the inside.

Please. Please. I want to see my Little Gray.

I will never stop looking for Little Gray. I search the elephants at each circus that works with ours, hoping to see her face, hoping for eyes like mine.

Never Again

I am trying to hide it, but I'm crying by the time we reach the other side of the tent, and Grandpa Bill comes limp-running behind. He makes his noise for *stop*, and the elephant does. Then he pets her, pats my knee, looks at me.

"She didn't mean to scare you, Lily," says Grandpa Bill. "There was a bee; I heard it, I saw it. I knew Queenie Grace was going to be scared, but there wasn't much I could do. I'm so sorry that happened, honey."

The audience is still going wild with excitement.

"Just wave at them like everything is fine," says my grandpa. "They can't see your eyes."

I do: I wave and pretend that it was all part of the act. Grandpa Bill whistles "Amazing Grace" and leads Queenie Grace out of the tent and into the back.

My heart is still hammering hard. I'm wheezing. This shimmery pink shirt is itchy. The circus life is obviously not for me. I see the bald twins, Harry and Larry looking with identical green eyes from a doorway; I see Trullia in her costume. The show must go on.

Grandpa stops Queenie Grace beside her painted trailer, parked in the fairgrounds, and she gets a long drink of water from a trough. He makes a stirrup of his hands and lifts me down to the ground.

"Whew," I say. "I'm never doing anything like that again."

I step back, way back, from the elephant.

Grandma Violet appears, white and purple hair flying around her face.

"It's okay, sweetheart," she says, hugging me. Her head comes exactly to my chest, right about where my heart is.

"Even something as big as an elephant has fear," says Grandma. "I bet she saw a bee. That's about the only thing that would make Queenie Grace take off like that."

"It *was* a bee," confirms Grandpa Bill. "Queenie Grace is still shook up. Look at her face."

"Let's walk her over to the lake and give her a bath," says Grandma Violet. "Cool her off. That always makes Queenie Grace happy. It's fine for us to leave for a little while. The big top's under control."

"Come on, Lily," says Grandpa. "It's fun to give her a bath.

Elephants love the water. Maybe she'd spray you, too, cool you off."

"No, thanks," I reply. "I'm . . . just going to go in and find my dad. I'm . . . kind of tired."

What I don't say—what I keep inside—is that I am even more terrified than before. I will never again ride an elephant, or be in a circus. I will never, ever take such a stupid chance again, *ever*. Pushing past fear and trying to be brave is just not worth it. And I will never, ever, in a million years be friends with Queenie Grace.

Queenie Grace Remembers December

It is already winter, December. I remember December. In one month of the wintertime, we live in Florida, in Gibtown, in this trailer park of other circus people and animals and amusement rides. Some retired; some not.

In Gibtown, there is a lion and some monkeys and three silly little dogs in frilly pink tutus next door. There is a rusted Ferris wheel and a crumbling silent carousel and an abandoned cotton candy stand. There is a fire-eating not-nice man and his kind wife, Mary the Bearded Lady, and my friend the Alligator Boy. This is where we all rest in December.

I am not made for snow, or for cold, so I am pleased to be here, in Florida, in Gibtown, where it smells warm and sweet like orange blossoms. I live in a field thick with flowers and grass, free to roam.

I love my vacation month. Bill always gives me a special gift for Christmas.

On this dusky Friday night, I see the colorful strands of lights draped from Bill and Violet's mobile home. Red and green twinkles, glimmers of hope. Through the window, I can see the tree, sparkly-light, shining very bright. I see my *mahout*, my sweet keeper—Bill the Giant. I see his tiny wife Violet.

Bill and Violet sometimes weep, especially at Christmastime, in Gibtown in December. They remember how much they miss the girl, their granddaughter, that odd girl Lily. They wish for something different for their daughter.

I know exactly how they feel.

Winter in West Virginia

It's December 22, only two more sleeps until Christmas Eve, and this is our baking day. We always make Rice Krispies Treats and peanut butter cookies. Tonight at seven, I will Skype with Grandpa Bill and Grandma Violet. Dad and I, we have our Christmas traditions, and I always know what to expect. I like a life with no surprises.

One day, I hope Trullia will explain. I want her to explain everything, like how and why she left us, and I'm going to ask her to explain what we ever did to force her to run away like that.

When elephants fly, maybe my mother will apologize. When elephants fly, maybe I'll forgive. Maybe. Maybe not.

The cabin is warm with the smell of butter and sugar. Cookies are cooling on paper towels. I love this Christmas baking day smell, plus the scent of the evergreen tree we cut from the mountain. The whole room feels cozy with cookies and Christmas. The tree is all lit up in the corner, decorated with every special ornament I've made since I was a baby. Dad is so proud of my art.

"Time to top off the tree," Dad says. He hands the shimmery star to me. My grandparents gave us this star when I was little.

"To light our way," I say, like always, carefully placing the star on the tip-top pointed branch of the tree. I arrange it nice and straight. It's always important to us that our star be just right.

Dad plugs the star into the strand of twinkle lights, and it gleams to life, shining.

"There," he says. "Now we can see through the dark. Find our way through another winter and back to summertime."

I love summer best, when everything is a riot of blossoms and blooms. My mother was named for a wildflower, and so am I. Lily Rose Pruitt, named for the common daylily that grows here on the mountain. I guess it's an appropriate name, because common daylilies are untamed and orange, and so is my hair. Not that anybody could have known that when I was born, a bald-headed baby that cried way too much and kept people awake at night.

I was born in summertime, when the mountain is full of flowers. They make me wheeze with my asthma, but I forgive them for that. After all, they're so beautiful and it's not their fault some people have allergies.

We have tall buttercup and jewelweed, touch-me-nots, Venus's looking glass and devil's paintbrush, purple goat's beard and fireweed. We're so exploding-full of flowers in the summertime that it almost makes your eyes go blind with beauty.

Sometimes I wonder how my mother could have left all these flowers, this mountain, our campground, my dad. But mostly I wonder how and why she could have left *me*. Her own flesh and blood and bones and breath.

And tonight, just like always, she won't even join in on the Skype call.

My grandparents' faces fill the computer screen, and their smiles beam sunshine. The wonder of Skype always makes them laugh. They look even older than the last time we Skyped, after a turkey dinner on Thanksgiving Day, but they are still really cute, in that old-people kind of way. Both with hair white as cotton (but Grandma's long and streaked with purple), and their eyes shine soft and blue.

"There you are, Lily-Bird!" says Grandma Violet. "Big

as life! West Virginia to Florida, and we're together again. Magic! Ta-da!"

"Hi!" says Grandpa Bill in his raspy voice. "How are you, Lily dear?"

"I'm fine."

"So good to see your face!" says Grandma Violet.

"So what do you want for Christmas?" asks Grandpa.

I shrug.

"Maybe new paints. A great year for me and Dad. To get good grades in school. That probably sounds like New Year's resolutions, but that's what I want."

"What a good girl!" says Grandma.

"A heart as big as West Virginia!" says Grandpa. They are full of compliments for me, that's for sure.

We never bring up my mother on these Skype visits. We act as if she doesn't even exist.

"So, uh, how's Florida?" I ask.

"Bright and sunny as ever!" says Grandpa. "Seventy degrees tonight."

"Wow," I say. "It's like below freezing here."

"One day, we're hoping you get down here to visit, sweetie," says Grandma. "Before you're all grown up."

"I know, right?" I reply. Dad's tapping my back. "Here, Dad wants to say hi."

Dad leans over my shoulder and puts his face in front of the screen.

"Hi!" he says, then steps away.

My grandparents laugh, and they both say "hi" at the same time.

"Let's see your tree, Lily," they say, like always. I carry the computer to the living room and show them the tree so they can ooh and aah.

"So sweet!" says Grandma. "Still using the star we gave you when you were a baby."

Then we chat about random things like school and how cool it is that Dad and I always make so many cookies and treats.

"Well, I'm beat," Grandpa says. He yawns. His face is pale. "Love you to the moon."

I look outside, through the living room window, at the frosty Friday night full moon hanging over our home in West Virginia. The same miraculous moon that shines over Florida, and my grandparents, and even over my mother.

"I love you, too," I say. "To the moon."

And I seriously do.

Queenie Grace Knows When Something Is Not Right

I am going to paint! I will paint Little Gray. Gray, gray, swish, gray. I love to paint.

Violet is inside baking. Bill sets my special easel up in the field. He gives me brushes and squirts of paint, circles of many colors I can choose to use.

"Paint away, Queenie Grace," he says. "I'll be mowing the yard."

Bill the Giant pats my back. He saunters away, a quick shuffle-shuffle limp-limp, wearing sneakers and torn shorts and a white T-shirt.

I smell the gasoline, hear the familiar putt-putt-putt. Bill pushes; tall grass disappears like magic. I love the smell of cut grass. Bill sings as he mows.

"'Amazing Grace,'" he sings loud and strong.

Twilight, Saturday sky streaked with purple and pink and blue. I add colors to my painting of Little Gray.

"How sweet the sound," Bill the Giant bellows.

But then there is no song. Something is wrong. My friend Bill has fallen. Bill lies on the ground. His face is down. The mower continues to putt.

I run. I try to push him up.

Bill, my keeper, my friend, my *mahout*, does not move. He lies still. But he is not sleeping.

Bill's face presses grass. I trumpet; I bellow; I wail. I push the running mower away from his face. I trumpet again.

I will not stop until someone comes to help!

This Bad News

Dad and I shiver outside and the sky snuggles up close to nighttime. It's December 23, Saturday, the day after our cookies and Skype. We always clean the wet dead leaves on this day, sweeping them from the mini-golf course. We bag and rake and rake and bag, collecting whatever is left from the fall. We get ready for wintertime, for the snow, for the never-ending darkness and the stubborn cold that we know will blow so nasty over our home.

"That wind is bitter," Dad says. His cheeks splotch red behind the rough stubble of beard.

"I know, right?"

"Let's get inside. I don't want you catching a cold."

We prop our rakes against the big, rickety wooden pirate ship that people walk through at the entrance to the golf course, sailing fast on their way to a good time. The pirate ship echoes empty at this time of the year. The wind blusters through it. If ships had wishes, this one would be wishing for summer, that's for sure.

"Now the grounds are all cleaned up and ready for Santa," Dad says, like always.

"Dad," I say. "I'm going to be thirteen. I don't believe."

"We all need to believe," Dad replies.

I just grin and go along with it, following Dad into the cabin.

I'm chowing down on a Rice Krispies Treat when Dad's cell phone rings. We've just put a pot of water on the stove to boil for hot chocolate.

"Magic Mountain Campground," Dad says in his business voice.

He listens. Dad's body stiffens; his eyes widen with surprise.

"Oh, my. Oh no. Oh, Violet," he says.

I stop chewing, sticky sweetness gluing my lips. The stove ticks; the water is getting hot.

"Okay," Dad says. "We'll get on Skype right away."

I swallow.

"What?" I ask. "What's wrong?"

Dad doesn't seem to hear me. He's standing at the kitchen table, flipping open his laptop and logging quickly in to Skype.

"What happened?" I ask.

"Grandma wants to tell you something," he says. "Sit down, honey."

Uh-oh. Sitting down is what you do for bad news.

I drag over a kitchen chair. It squeaks and complains across the floor. Grandma's face fills the screen. Her hair flies wild around her face; her eyes bulge puffy and red. Her mouth is turned down, and everything about her seems to sag.

"Where's Grandpa?" I ask, breathing fast.

"Honey, Grandpa had a heart attack tonight." Grandma pauses, licks her lips, looks down. "He's gone, sweetheart. Grandpa Bill died."

I am frozen to the chair, shocked. *Am I dreaming this?*

"How? When? Why?" Three words: that's all I can say. My own heart is attacking my body, hammering like something mad and alive.

Grandma Violet dissolves. She starts to cry.

"Nobody knows how or why. I don't know what time. This doesn't even feel real."

"No way! No! He was fine, just last night, right? He was . . . fine." I'm so confused.

"He was," replies Grandma, "and then he wasn't."

My heart falls like a dropped ball, bounces uncontrollably around the floor. The water on the stove is bubbling furiously, crazily trying to escape the pot.

I look at Dad. Tears dribble down his face, tracing slow, awkward paths through the beard stubble. He puts his arm around my shoulders, draws me close.

"We will see him again," says Grandma, "in heaven."

"But . . . that's so far away!" I say. "Too long to wait."

"I know, honey," says Grandma. "But sometimes we just have no say. We just have to wait. It's not up to us."

I nod and blink. I don't want to cry on Skype. I've got to be strong for my grandma.

"It's okay to cry, hon," Grandma says. "That's what we need to do when someone we love leaves. We need to get it out."

And so I do. I let go and I weep. I don't know what I'm going to do without my grandpa in my life.

Dad goes to turn off the stove, dumps the boiling water in the sink. Nobody cares about hot chocolate at a time like this. It can't fix a thing.

"I love you to the moon," says Grandma before we sign off.

"Love you, too," I say. My voice breaks, shatters like a fallen lightbulb. "Love Grandpa, too."

And then I start to sob again, as if this bad news is once again brand-new.

The Giant Has Died

The Giant has died and I cry. Elephants do cry.

I tried, I really tried to keep him alive.

I pushed the lawn mower away from Bill so that it would not run over him. The smell of gasoline and cut grass; the *putt-putt* of the mower; those things stick in my mind like taffy.

I tried to gently lift the Giant with my trunk. He did not move. I nuzzled him. He did not move. I nudged him gently with one hoof. He still did not move. His skin looked white-blue, like milk, like the moon. I trumpeted, loudly. *Help! Come! Quickly! Hurry!*

I rumbled. I ran. I stampeded until Violet and Trullia came, and then the winter camp neighbors, and then the ambulance with frantic red flashing lights and screaming siren. I wailed when I heard Violet say that he was gone.

But the Giant, he lost his life tonight. I lost my owner, my trainer, my keeper, my *mahout*. I lost everything—everything! That is why I refuse to move from this spot, behind the silver trailer with its blinking happy lights, in the big grassy field with the purple wildflowers and yellow weeds. My grief will keep me here, where I last saw the Giant. I can smell him still, my best friend Bill.

Bill the Giant. He had a large heart, too, and that heart killed him in the end.

They took him away in the ambulance, but I can still smell him. The scent of his skin, the salt; it lingers on my trunk.

Oh, I miss my Bill. I am alone. I am so, so alone.

A Big Decision

I sleep in until ten the next morning, on this Christmas Eve Sunday. The sky hangs gray; not much difference between night and morning. For a split second, I forget about last night and the bad news. But then I remember again. That's the problem with waking up: eventually you remember.

"Good morning, sleepyhead," Dad says when I blunder into the kitchen in pink flannel pajamas, my eyes full of sleep and grouchy denial.

"Morning," I mumble. "It's not exactly 'good.'"

"Every day, no matter how sad, has *something* good in it," Dad says. He cracks eggs into a red bowl.

I just shrug, shake my head, bite the inside of my cheek hard so that I don't start to cry. That's a trick I learned when

I was little. Keep the pain on the *inside*.

"I have something for you to think about, Lily," Dad says. "It's a big decision, but unfortunately you have to make it pretty quick." He whips the eggs, puts butter in the frying pan, turns on the stove. Sizzle fills the room.

"What?" I sink down into a kitchen chair, running my hands through the tangles in my hair.

"Well, here's the thing, Lily. Grandma called early this morning, and she's thinking about the funeral. She'd really like for you to be there, and so she found a great deal on holiday airfare on some website. She'd pay half and I can cover the other half, but you'd have to fly today."

"*Today?*"

Dad nods. He pours the eggs into the hot butter, stirs, scrambles.

"Grandma's all ready with her credit card as soon as you give her the word. I can get you to the airport in less than an hour. You'd have to pack your bag pretty quick. We'd stop first and get you a cell phone—"

"My own phone?"

"Just one with minutes for a texting plan. Like, to keep in touch with quick stuff. Or for emergencies."

What other kind of emergency could possibly happen? My grandpa already died.

"So I know you've never flown, sweetheart, and I'm really

sorry that I can't afford to get myself a ticket, too. But I know you'll be fine! You're a smart girl and you're brave."

"I'm so not brave!"

"You're smart. And you have a great big heart. And that great big heart is exactly what Grandma Violet needs right now."

"But . . . what about Christmas? It's Christmas Eve!" I pick at a little rip in the plastic tablecloth, making it bigger.

"I know," Dad says. "And I'll save it for you. Some things can wait. Even your favorite holiday."

I look at the tree. I look at the star. I look at the plates of cookies and treats, made by Dad and me. I look at the wrapped gifts under the tree.

"Promise? You promise to wait?"

"You can count on me," my dad says.

And I know I can. Dad pours me a big glass of orange juice, puts some eggs on a plate for me, and hands me the bottle of ketchup.

"How long do I have to decide?" I ask.

"Take a little walk after you eat breakfast and think about it," Dad says. "And whatever you decide will be fine."

Trudging up one of our hiking trails, I'm thinking and thinking and thinking. But what if my mother is mean to me? What if the elephant charges me or smothers me? What if

I'm scared, all alone, way up high in the sky? What if I get lost? What if I can't figure out the airport? What if the plane crashes? What if Dad has a heart attack while I'm gone? What if, what if, what if? My entire mind has turned into one big question mark.

I've never been on an airplane. I've never gone anywhere alone. I'm twelve. I know nothing about flying or Florida or funerals. I've never even *been* to a funeral!

What to do, what to do, what to do? That's what I'm thinking with each crunch of my boot against frozen ground, with every crackle of dead leaves, with every snap of tree limb that I break with my steps. The air is so cold that the tiny hairs freeze inside my nose, and it feels as though I'm frozen from the inside out.

What should I do?

And then I remember how Grandpa Bill saved my life when I was six. I remember how it felt to be cuddled in his arms. I remember how he'd blow bubbles for me, and we'd see each other's faces through the bubbles as I looked up. I remember how he was always there for me when my mother was not.

"Yes," I say out loud, to the hard ground and to the bare-limbed trees and to the quiet gray sky.

"Yes, I'll go. I'll be there, Grandpa Bill. I'll be there for you. And I'll try to be brave."

And then I jump as a bird startles me, flapping its wings on the branch of a tree. I gasp, then almost laugh.

The bird flies away, into the West Virginia winter sky, leaving me behind to finally make up my mind.

"I'm going to fly, too," I call after the bird. "Just like you."

Maybe Queenie Grace
Can Die, Too

It is Sunday morning. Violet lugs bucket after bucket of water from the hose. She dumps them, sloshing the water into my trough. She does not speak. The Giant always had words, sometimes song. It was as if his spirits rose with the sun.

I am not thirsty. I am not hungry. I do not want the carrot she offers. I do not like the taste of Violet's hand in my water. I long for Bill. Where is Bill? Where do people go when they leave their bodies?

Violet looks up at me. She meets my eyes with hers.

"I miss him, too, you know," she says. Her voice is a whisper.

The daughter, Trullia, rambles outside of the trailer. She walks with the man Mike, who smells of secrets and sneakiness. They go to the car, and they drive away.

The fire-eating man, Charlie, comes out of his trailer. He settles into his rocking chair, staring at me and smoking his smelly cigar. His wife, Mary the Bearded Lady, comes outside, too. She strokes her beard; he smokes.

"Such a shame," she says. "I always liked Bill."

Charlie takes his cigar from his mouth, points it at me.

"It was the elephant," he says. "That darn elephant probably killed him. I always told Bill that elephant would be the death of him yet."

"Oh," says Mary, "Queenie Grace wouldn't hurt a flea."

Charlie just stares at me, his eyes mean and hard under his cowboy hat. Charlie has a beard, bushy and black like his wife's. Charlie makes my skin quiver.

"We need to get that critter out of Gibtown," he says, "before it hurts somebody else."

I hang my head. I agree with Mary: I would not harm a flea.

I stand sad and scared in this place, in the spot where I last saw my friend. The ground flattened hopelessly where he fell. I will not move. I refuse food. I will not drink.

I sway, shift my weight, weave, rock. Tears fall, and the salt of them drops into my water.

Maybe I can die, too.

I'm Not in
West Virginia Anymore

The airplane rises into the sky and I swear, I'm afraid that I might just die. How can all this weight—all these people—*fly?* It's a five o'clock flight; outside (and inside), it looks like night.

I'm sitting beside a nice yellow-haired lady with sparkly earrings and a refreshing smell of mint. She wears these cat's-eye glasses with green sequins, and a lot of blush, which makes her look excited. She squeezes my hand when she sees how nervous I am, and the skin of her hand is soft like flowers at the end of summer.

I'm in the window seat, and she's squished between me and a frowning serious businessman who's obsessed with his work. So Donna and I are stuck with each other. She lives in Florida . . . was visiting somebody in West Virginia, she says.

"That winter weather, brrrrrrr," she says, hugging herself and making a fake shiver.

"I know. We're always waiting for summer to come once again."

"So where are you going, honey?" the lady asks. She's holding a magazine, and it's open, but she's paying attention to me. I'm sketching in my notebook, which is what I do when I'm nervous.

"Florida, a place called Gibtown. My grandfather died, so I have to go to the funeral."

"Oh, I'm so sorry, sweetheart." The old lady pats my arm, which just about does it for me. I have to bite the inside of my cheek and repeat inside my mind: *I will not cry, I will not cry, I will not cry. . . .*

"Grief won't last forever, honey," Donna says. "It'll go through stages, like a roller-coaster ride, and you just have to hold on and go with it. I promise, though, that you'll heal one day. It'll never go away, but it will be different."

I try to change the subject, because talking about death isn't my favorite thing.

"This airplane is bumpy," I say. I close my notebook and put my pencil in my pocket.

The lady is still holding my hand and she's still on the subject of death.

"So is this is your mother's father or your father's father who passed?" she asks.

"Um, my mother's dad."

"Your mother isn't coming with you to the funeral?"

"Well, um, she's already there. She's been traveling with a circus since I was three."

I get all choked up at the last part of the sentence, and Donna leans over and presses her cheek to mine.

"Oh, sometimes in life those things happen," she says. "We just have to learn to forgive and keep on living. Let go of fear, trust that everything will be peachy. And if not peachy, at least *good enough*. Good enough for us!"

I nod. I glance down at the open pages of Donna's glossy magazine. There's a big headline that says *YOU CAN DO IT! MOVE FORWARD WITH LOVE! SPREAD YOUR WINGS AND FLY!!!!*

That's way too many exclamation points for me at this time of my life.

The airplane is landing. It's quivery, and I'm holding my breath, squeezing the seat arms with each hand. Donna circles my wrist, stroking my skin with her fingers, and once again I have to bite the inside of my cheek. *Keep it inside.* That's my motto.

Coming back to earth is scary. It's noisy and it feels like the airplane isn't going to stop and my stomach drops and my heart skitters. Donna hands me a little snack pack of peanuts, and I take them but don't open the bag, just shove them into the pocket of my jacket.

Finally, the plane screeches to a stop. We all unclick our seat belts, stand, yawn, and stretch. I reach up and grab my small black suitcase from the overhead compartment. My suitcase does not have wheels, because apparently my dad is old-fashioned like that. All I see through the airplane window is darkness, and airport workers, and blinking red lights.

"Bye, sweetheart," says Donna. "I'll be thinking of you."

She hands me a card, a flowery one with her name and phone number and the words *Spiritual Adviser & Animal Communicator*.

I read the card out loud.

"That's an . . . unusual job," I say.

"Well, people have unusual lives!" replies Donna. "Like, for example, you. Your mother works in a circus, and you have a different living situation. Sometimes people just need some spiritual advice! And animals . . . well, they need communication, too."

I nod.

"Okay," I say.

"Call me if you need anything," she says. "Here, write down your number, too."

She has me write my cell number on another of her cards, and then she tucks it in her wallet like something precious.

We give each other an awkward quick hug, and I take the phone from my pocket. I text Dad.

Here.

His text comes right back, as if he was just waiting for mine.

Great. Be safe. Love you.

Love you, too.

Lugging the suitcase, I follow the other people through a tunnel-like ramp, and, when I trudge from the other end, into the too-bright and busy airport filled with important people coming and going, and walk all the way to the baggage claim, there she is: Trullia Lee Pruitt, in the flesh, standing with some bald-headed neck-tattoo guy. Her hair is dyed blond, but with roots the color of mine, and her eyes are lined with so much makeup that she looks fake. Her lips are pink and plumped up.

"Lily!" she calls, waving like Miss America, teetering on high heels. (Trullia's always a bit more show-offy and fake-cheery when she has a new boyfriend.) They come running like we're long-lost friends, and the bald man takes my suitcase. His hand feels rough when it brushes against mine.

"Hey," he says. "I'm Mike."

He smells like cigarette smoke and he's missing some teeth, plus he's wearing a dirty white undershirt, but it's pretty nice that he relieved me of the suitcase weight. Even if it does mean he has to lift his arm, which results in the disgusting smell of sweat coming from that gross hairy underarm.

My mother gives me a halfhearted, one-armed hug. She smells like smoke, too, plus onions. The mothers in my dream world smell like sugar cookies and roses, and they dress snazzy yet classy, like the moms in the Old Navy Christmas commercials. This is real life, though, not my made-up one, and Trullia Pruitt is wearing a short blue sundress that's like two sizes too small.

"I can't even believe it about Grandpa," I say.

"I know," Trullia says. "It doesn't feel real to me, either."

There's a minute of awkward silence.

"And I can't believe you're thirteen!" Trullia finally says, stepping back to study me head to toe. She hasn't seen me since summer, so I guess I've changed.

"I'm twelve. I'll be thirteen in the summer. July twenty-third."

Trullia just brushes it off, as if she forgot my age on purpose.

"Wow," she says. "You sure are getting tall. Taller than me!"

Yeah, I think. *That's what happens when you're not looking.*

Stepping out through the airport doors feels like walking into the rainforest part of the little zoo back home: all steamy and heavy and warm. It's as if a damp wool blanket has been thrown all over the whole world, and I break out in a sweat. Cars honk, people hurry, suitcases roll and clatter. I can't even see any stars. The sky is dark. It must be after eight o'clock, I know, but otherwise I've lost all track of time.

"There's our car." Trullia points to a little beaten-up car that's parked all crooked.

"How far is the trailer park?" I ask.

"Not far," says Mike. "Be there before you know it."

The entire time in the car, Trullia blah-blah-blahs in that scratchy cigarette-torn voice of hers, mostly about how Grandpa Bill was just mowing the yard and everything was normal and fine and then he just went. *Boom.* Just like that.

I gaze through the window, into the darkness. I am like the wheels of this car, missing my hubcap: Dad.

"Queenie Grace is amazing," Trullia says. "She tried to save Dad. It's so sad." Her voice quivers.

"The elephant was just following her wild instinct," Mike says. "Trying to move the body."

"No," Trullia says, her voice firm. "She was trying to save my dad."

Mike takes a pack of cigarettes from the pocket of his shirt. He shakes one out, taps it against his wrist, driving with one hand. Then he casually sticks that cigarette in his mouth.

"Um, I'm allergic to cigarette smoke," I say, and Trullia

turns to look at me as if she blames me for that.

I cough, just to show them that even the sight of a cigarette can get me going.

"I'll save it for later," Mike says, a wisp of annoyance tickling his voice, tucking the cigarette behind his ear.

"Thanks."

"Don't mention it."

Trullia turns around to look at me, grinning as if this new boyfriend of hers is all that.

"You can take off that jacket, Lily," she says. "You're not in West Virginia anymore."

I shrug off the jacket. Trullia's window is open, and my hair blows. The air smells fishy and deep. I am drowning in neon. Flashing signs greet us, saying *Drive Your Own Race Car* and *Pawnshop* and *Cheap Wine* and *Beer.* Far as I can tell from here, Florida is not all it's cracked up to be.

"Do you ever see alligators?" I ask.

"Sure," says Mike. "Do you see bears in West Virginia?"

"Sometimes," I say, "if you're lucky."

"Same here," Mike replies. "Things are really mostly the same all over, I suppose."

"We're almost home," Trullia says. "There's our landmark: the giant boot!"

We pass a statue . . . of a gigantic boot.

"Ooo-kay," I say. "Why is there a statue of a boot?"

"That's a replica of the original Giant's boot: size twenty-two," replies Mike. "Your grandfather was related to that guy, supposedly."

"We're kind of famous in Gibtown," Trullia adds as the car pushes forward.

"You have big shoes to fill, Lily," says Mike.

The car rattles along a road full of potholes. Gibtown is just a bunch of concrete buildings, rows and rows of mobile homes decorated with Christmas stuff, and lots of junk scattered everywhere. There's a battered little restaurant with signs that say *Fishing Camp Eatery* and *We Sell Worms*.

"Welcome to Gibtown," says Mike, "where life is a circus every day."

"Hey!" says Trullia. "I grew up here! I love it."

"I didn't mean it as an insult," Mike insists.

In the flicker of some dim streetlights, I see an old merry-go-round with carousel horses, a Ferris wheel looming up into the night, a couple of lonely bumper cars, an abandoned cotton candy stand.

"Why are there rides?" I ask. "Do they actually work?"

"Most of them are just stored here," says Trullia. "Old and broken-down, like most of the people."

Mike and Trullia crack up.

"And the animals," Trullia adds. "Most of them are pretty old and broken, too."

"What kind of animals?" I ask. "I know I've seen tigers

and a bear and some dogs, when I go to the circus."

"Oh, plenty of animals that don't even work in the circus anymore," says Mike. "There's a couple of ancient monkeys a few doors down. Plus these three annoying yippy white poodles that wear tutus. Oh, and there are a bunch of retired leopards."

"Ooo-kay," I say. "I hope they're in cages."

"Nope. No cages in Gibtown."

"So . . . it's actually *legal* to keep big wild animals here? Just loose?"

"Yup," says Mike. "Gibtown's the only place in America classified as RSB: residential show business zone. That means circus folks can train grizzly bears in their front yard, keep an elephant, a pet tiger, have a Ferris wheel out back."

"So do you work for the circus, too?"

"Yep. I'm a ruffie. I set up the shows and games. Sometimes I work two days straight, then pack up and move on to the next town. Only time we take a break is in December, when we all come here to Gibtown. Some call it Showtown. Others call it the strangest town in the nation. We have a gas station, library, bar, tattoo shop, grocery store, pharmacy, and trapeze school."

"Is there anybody my age?"

"Well," says Trullia, thinking, "there is Henry Jack. He's about twelve, I think. His skin is wrinkled like an alligator's."

"Seriously?" I ask.

"Yup."

Mike presses on the brake, which is screechy, and I almost shriek, because limping slowly right across the road in front of the car is a lion. A wild *lion!*

"There goes good old Boldo," says Mike. "Poor thing's on his last legs, so he's pretty slow."

"Hello, Boldo," Trullia croons through the open window.

I watch the lion go, and all I can think is that I wish I were home.

The lion disappears and Mike drives between an inflatable light-up snowman and a big vinyl snow dome that sways slightly in the night.

"Here we are," he says. "There's the neighbor guy, Fire-Eating Charlie, just doing his thing."

I look to my right, and a man in a cowboy hat is all lit up by a flaming stick of fire. He tips back his head and the fire goes out. Then he turns to look across the yard, and even in the dark I can tell that his eyes meet mine.

I shiver. The fire-eater creeps me out. In the window of the trailer behind him, three white poodles are yipping and yapping, leaping at the glass.

"Shut up!" somebody yells.

I look to my left and there's Grandpa Bill's elephant, outlined huge and shadowy against the night. I shudder.

"Welcome home," says Trullia Lee Pruitt.

The Girl Lily Is Here

The girl is here. Lily. Bill's little one, the anxious child we see when we're on the road. Wavy hair like the curled, peeled skin of tangerines. Speckled face. Eyes shadowy as a sky getting ready to storm. A sad smell of fear and loneliness. Her heart thrashes extra hard, and I can hear it from here.

She steps gingerly out into the grass from the back of the car, and the scent is extra strong. This girl Lily does not trust, and her nervousness hangs on her like a ripped dress.

"Say hello to Queenie Grace," Trullia says. "You'll probably have to go to her because she's not moving."

"No, thanks," says the girl. "I'm . . . kind of scared of elephants, you know."

"Oh, I know," says Trullia. "And there really is no reason

for it. No reason at all. Queenie Grace would never hurt you."

Mike flicks his lighter, holds a cigarette to the flame, puts it in his mouth. He blows smoke. I can smell it. I do not enjoy the smell of cigarette smoke. It smells gray, but not gray like me. Gray like danger. This man Mike is a threat.

The girl does not look at me. She does not speak to me. Lily has hunched shoulders and tired eyes. She carries a thick padded black jacket, and heavy fur boots are on her feet. Jeans, tight to her legs. She is thin, too thin, legs like sticks. I will paint her one day, and all I will need are lines. Slashes and lines, dark, angry, melancholy.

Violet bursts through the door. She spreads her arms wide, as if to fly. This is the happiest face she has worn in a while.

"Lily-Bird!" she calls.

The girl is not a bird. She does not have wings; she cannot fly. The sky is not her home, and neither is the winter camp. She does not belong here. She is longing for *her* home, for *her* family.

I smell peanuts, salty, salty peanuts. My mouth waters, I swing my trunk. I sway, I shift my weight, I weave. I heave out a sound, and the girl glances back over her shoulder.

Our eyes meet, finally, just one glimpse, but then it is time for the people to go inside.

This Place Is Crazy

Grandma Violet comes running, bounding along pretty fast for a grandma. She wraps me up in a snug two-armed hug that feels like love. I must have grown since summer, because now her head doesn't even reach my heart.

"Oh, honey!" she says, and I hear tears in her voice.

"I'm sorry about Grandpa," I say, and she really breaks down.

"I know," Grandma says. "Me too."

We hug for a long time, and then she steps back, studying me.

"Lily, my girl," Grandma keeps saying. "You are growing up so fast! You've gotten so tall!"

Inside the trailer, it smells like smoke, and socks, and old people, plus something like French fries or a hamburger.

There's a tree—a green plastic bare one—but nothing else with a hint of Christmas. One saggy green sofa, two black recliners, a tiny red kitchen with a miniature silver refrigerator. Pictures on the walls of my grandma and grandpa, looking happy and young. There are my school pictures, too, framed in gold, and old photos of Trullia. There's even a picture of way-young Trullia and my dad at their high school prom, back before they moved to West Virginia and had me. And of course there are lots of pictures of Trullia on the flying trapeze: Miss Famous.

A cuckoo clock chirps nine times.

"Welcome to our little home, Lily," says Grandma. "It's not fancy, but it's ours. And it's a little bigger than that motor home we travel in."

My grandma waves her hand, which is wrinkly and spotted brown like most people who are in their sixties. She is so teeny and fragile; her purple-streaked hair hangs almost to her waist. Grandma Violet's face is crinkly and kind, and she's wearing plaid shorts and red Converse shoes (just like mine!) with a black T-shirt that says *Be Yourself.* I have to admit: my grandmother is pretty hip, with that purple hair and cool clothing.

"So how was the flight, Lily-Bird?" asks Grandma.

"Okay," I say. "I sat with a nice lady. Her name was Donna, and she wore these funky cat's-eye glasses and she was a 'spiritual adviser and animal communicator' of some kind."

"That's good," Grandma says. "It always makes flying nicer when you have a friend. Plus, who doesn't need a little bit of spiritual advice and communication with animals, every now and then?"

"Man, this suitcase is heavy," complains Mike, scrunching up his face as if he's lifting weights. "Where can I put this thing?"

"Oh, just set it down anywhere," says Grandma. "Make yourself at home, Lily. Our home is your home, too."

"You can take off those boots," says Trullia. "You keep forgetting: you're not in West Virginia anymore."

Mike puts my suitcase on the sofa.

"Feels like she packed the entire state of West Virginia," he says.

"Did you pack a swimsuit?" asks Trullia. "There's a pool."

"Um . . . no. I kind of forgot. It was just so cold when I left home that I didn't even think about swimming."

"I understand how that happens," says Grandma. "It's like when I'm here in Florida, I can't even imagine it snowing and being cold in West Virginia. Two different worlds. How's your father, Lily?"

"Good. He's good."

My mother obviously doesn't like talking about my dad. She chews on a fingernail, and then she changes the subject.

"Mom!" says Trullia. "Where are the tree ornaments? Where are the lights?"

"I took the ornaments down," Grandma says. "I wrapped up the lights. Who feels like celebrating now?"

"That's kind of extreme," Trullia says.

"I just needed to do something while you were gone, so I undecorated the tree," Grandma says.

"But you didn't take down the outside lights?" Trullia asks.

Grandma shrugs. "Can't explain it," she says. "I'm just not feeling the holiday spirit."

"Well, we do have Lily here," says Trullia. "We could do it for her."

No. Don't do anything for me. Please. Because that would mean I have to appreciate, and I'm not in an appreciation kind of mood, to tell you the truth.

"This is Christmas Eve," says Mike. "You need a freaking tree."

"I have a dang tree," says Grandma. "And that's all I have."

They've moved Trullia to the green sofa, and Mike to the recliner, and given me their room, which really isn't much to brag about. A creaky whining bed that sags in the middle; a dresser with broken drawers. Apparently, everything in this trailer is broken or old or tired or sad.

It's only nine thirty, but I'm tired. Too sleepy to even unpack my suitcase and take out my pajamas. Flying wore me out. It's like I've left my entire body and half my mind in the sky.

I flop into the bed, lying on top of the covers.

Grandma Violet made macaroni and cheese with hot dogs for my dinner, but I'm still kind of hungry. That's when I remember the pack of peanuts in my jacket pocket.

I take out the peanuts, rip open the pack, and munch a few. But then I get thirsty. I really don't want to go back out and talk to anyone. I decide to just suck it up and go to sleep. I put the pack of peanuts on top of the dresser.

I turn off the light and through the window, I can see the elephant, a hulking shadow in the night. It's a little bit cool tonight, so the windows are closed. I can imagine the sounds of her huffy breathing, though.

I yank off my jeans, drop them on the floor, and climb once again into the complaining bed, wearing the shirt and socks from this morning. So weird to think that I put these clothes on just this morning, at home, with my dad nearby. And now here I am: same clothes, same me, same moon overhead . . . but somehow everything has changed.

Good night. Going to bed, I text Dad, and he texts right back.

Sweet dreams. Love you.

I wish he was here to tuck me in, to sing one of his silly songs, to read a book with me. I know I'm kind of old for all that, but still.

I just really love my dad.

Falling asleep, I think I'm in a dream, something about tapping and knocking. Then a crash, a huge splintering sound of breaking glass, and I sit up. It's real. The glass of the window is crashed, a big, jagged, sharp, star-shaped hole letting in a piece of the night.

"What the . . . ?"

And then I see it: the trunk of the elephant, reaching boldly into the room, eating from the open pack of peanuts I left on the dresser.

It's Queenie Grace, and she just keeps eating the peanuts, never taking one eye from my face.

I don't know what to do, so I don't do anything. I just sit and stare, knees and blanket to my chin, quivering. The clock in the living room cuckoos twelve times, and I reach over and turn on the light.

The elephant is bleeding. She has a small spot of blood on her trunk, and then it's dripping onto the broken old dresser in this creepy little room.

This feels like a nightmare, some crazy bad dream, but then I know I'm awake because Trullia Lee Pruitt busts hollering into the room.

She goes straight to the elephant, never mind me, and then she yells for my grandmother and for Mike, and before you know it, there's a big ruckus going on.

I'm watching them all through the broken window, trying not to step in shards of broken glass that fell on the bedroom floor.

"What are you going to disinfect it with?" Trullia asks.

"Hydrogen peroxide," Grandma says.

"Are you sure that's the right thing to use?" Trullia asks, and it strikes me that she worries more about the elephant than she does about me.

"Yes," Grandma says.

"I bet it'll burn," Trullia says.

"Babe," Mike says, "it's an elephant. Just an elephant. Chill out a little bit, okay?"

From here I can see that Trullia's gnawing on her fingernails again.

Grandma pours hydrogen peroxide on the elephant's trunk and Trullia helps to hold it still. The elephant makes noise as Grandma Violet wraps gauze around the cut on its trunk.

Mike carries a big chain across the yard.

"Oh, I don't know about that, Mike," Grandma says.

"Well, we can't have her breaking windows and stuff," Mike replies.

Grandma sighs. I can see the rise and fall of her chest with her deep breath.

"I'm too tired to fight," Grandma says.

Mike bends down and ties the chain around one of Queenie Grace's legs, then he circles a tree with the chain. He knots it tight and steps back, surveying the elephant and the chain.

"That should keep her safe for the night," Mike says. "And keep *us* safe."

"She only wanted the peanuts," I whisper to myself, kind of surprised that I'm feeling half-sorry for the elephant.

I smell cigar smoke. The creepy fire-eater is standing outside, gawking and smoking. I swear he catches my eye again, even through the darkness.

I look away. The elephant stares at me, too.

I know just how Queenie Grace feels; I do. But this much, too, is true: I still don't like her. After all, that elephant did try to kill me one time, and she scared the heck out of me back in July.

Maybe the chains serve her right.

Queenie Grace Is in Trouble

I am in trouble, big trouble. They have chained me, all because I ate the peanuts. I have never before been chained in this place. Bill the Giant would never, ever chain me.

It is morning; I am still confined by the chain. Violet brings my water; she does not speak. Trullia brings my food; I will not eat. I will teach them how to treat an elephant.

I wish I could paint. I wish I could do my tricks. I wish it was summer, and the circus was my life. I wish that my best friend Bill would come back and take off the chain.

I wish that the girl Lily would just go away. She is to blame for leaving the peanuts where I could see. The girl was teasing me. I wish she would just go home, where she belongs, and I wish that everything wrong would turn right.

I wish that Saturday had never turned to night. I wish

the Giant had not decided to mow the grass. I wish that his heart had been stronger.

I wonder how long I will remain on this chain.

This day feels like a year. It feels like forever.

I will never be okay again.

A Christmas Tizzy

It's Christmas—Monday morning—and the elephant keens and whines outside. There's no way you can get away from the racket.

Grandma Violet is making French toast for breakfast. Mike sleeps on the recliner; Trullia's snoozing on the sofa. They both snore. I'm sitting on the floor, trying to block out the noise of elephant with the TV.

The elephant just keeps going with her sad sounds.

Birds chirp outside and the sky is bright, but inside it's dim and quiet and thick with grief. No joy to the world in here. More like, *Let's open this stuff and get it over with so we can all go back to being sad and alone.*

I open the first one, crumple the wrapping paper, and

shove it into the trash bag Grandma brought into the living room.

"A set of watercolors!" I say. "Awesome. Thank you."

"You're welcome," Grandma says. "Here's another one from me."

She hands me a big package.

I pull off the snowman paper. It's brushes, an easel, and canvases.

"Cool," I say. "Now I can paint, here in Florida."

Trullia hands me a gift. I open it. A coloring book and Crayola crayons.

"Look, it's all wildflowers!" she says, as if I can't see that. "It's like you and me, Lily. Wildflowers. That's us."

"Why'd you get her a little-kid coloring book?" Mike asks. "She's too big for that."

"Nobody's too old for coloring!" Trullia says. "My therapist recommends it! It's great stress relief."

Mike just shakes his head.

She hands me another one, wrapped in paper that says *Happy Birthday*. I open it: pink flip-flops with sparkly sequins and a flowery dress.

"You'll be a teenager next year, and we need to get you looking stylish," Trullia says. "Plus, you need something decent to wear for the funeral."

I look at her. Trullia's eyes are red, smeared with sleep and mascara.

"Thank you," I say. These might be my first-ever gifts from my mother, at least as far back as I can remember.

"And last, but not least, one from me," says Mike. He hands me a package wrapped in newspaper. I open it. It's a Rainbow Loom, to make rubber band bracelets.

"Now you can make a bracelet for everybody in Gibtown!" Mike says.

"Thank you," I say, even though I have no desire to make rubber band bracelets.

"Nice to make Christmas fun for a kid," Mike says. "I never had that. Nobody ever cared enough."

"That's sad," I say, but then he changes the subject.

"Open it up," he says. "Check it out."

Grandma and Trullia ooh and aah over the Rainbow Loom. They are all acting in that fake perky way that adults put on whenever they're actually super sad. It's as if the outside totally clashes with the inside, like trying to match plaid with stripes. It kind of hurts my eyes to look at them, so false and full of pretend life.

Thank you, thank you, thank you. At least I'm polite. My dad taught me right.

We are sitting down to a noon Christmas dinner, all four of us squished around the tiny table in the teeny kitchen. There's ham and peas and Stovetop stuffing and potato rolls. Nobody said grace. Nobody's talking, just eating. Grandma's eyes are puffy, and Trullia still hasn't washed the smudged makeup from her face. Mike is sweating, beads of perspiration snaking down his cheeks.

"You two should think about getting rid of that elephant," Mike says out of the blue.

Grandma Violet raises her eyes from her plate to Mike's face, and they cut sharp like a knife.

"Don't even say that, not even as a joke," she snaps. "Bill would never have gone for that."

"Well, what if it keeps acting up and hurts somebody? What if you can't afford to keep it, to feed it, now that the act can't happen?"

"Maybe it'll just have to be the Amazing Queenie Grace and Her Best Friend, Violet," Grandma says. She spoons peas into her mouth, swallowing what she *really* wants to say.

"Mom, you know that you and Queenie Grace will never click like Dad did with her," says Trullia, looking up with her shadowed eyes.

"How about the Amazing Queenie Grace and Her Best Friend, Mike?" asks Mike. He wipes his forehead with his paper napkin.

"*Pfffft.* Queenie Grace doesn't even like you," Trullia says.

"Probably likes me more than it likes you," retorts Mike.

"Stop bickering, you two!" says Grandma Violet. "Set an example for Lily here. And no more discussion about

Queenie Grace, please, not until later. It's just too over-whelming right now."

"I feel so bad for Queenie Grace," Trullia says. "I know exactly how she feels. She feels empty. And confused. And mad. And sad. All wrapped up in one big fat package."

Grandma nods.

"You don't have to be human to feel grief," she says.

Trullia pushes away from the table. Still in her chair, she pulls back the little white curtain to peer out the kitchen window.

"Where the heck is Queenie Grace, anyway?" she says. "She's not out there!"

Trullia lets the curtain fall back, presses both hands to her head.

"She's got to be out there!" Mike says, dropping his fork. "I chained her tight to the tree!"

Mike and Trullia both stand, pushing each other to be the first at the living room window. They remind me of two toddlers in a crowded day care, both of them brats.

My grandmother hops up and runs outside, her long hair flying behind.

"She's not out here," she hollers from the little porch. Grandma shades her eyes, looks left and right, frantic.

"Queenie Grace!" she yells, like calling a dog. "Queenie Grace!" The yippy little poodles next door are yapping their heads off.

"Where could she be?" shrieks Trullia.

"I have no idea," my grandma shouts from the porch, and she's a silhouette against the blinding bright blue Florida sky. "Who knows? As far as an elephant can run."

"No way!" says Trullia. "This can't be happening!"

"Call 911," says my grandma. "We need to find her. What if she runs out on the road?"

My grandma dashes into the yard, and Trullia and Mike both turn and bump into each other, like on a funny TV show. These three are all in a tizzy about the runaway elephant, and so they don't even notice me as I run outside.

I just sprint past Grandma, veer to the left, and dash fast past the home of creepy Charlie the fire-eating weirdo. My Converse sneakers slap the black pavement, forward, forward. I can obviously run much faster than those three old people, who are freaking out so loud I can still hear them.

I'm going to find that elephant.

Queenie Grace Is Free of the Chains

It is early morning, and I am free of the chains! I broke them because there was an insect. It was a buzzing yellow jacket, and I did not want to be stung.

So now I am running.

I am afraid, as if the entire world has turned into one big buzzing bee. I am scared of being without Bill, scared of having nowhere to go, scared of leaving my home. I can feel my heart inside of me.

I run. I thunder past the yipping little dogs and the sleeping lion and the climbing monkey. I run past the quiet trailers. People are noticing, coming out on their porches, staring. Some yell. I run past the things that are no longer used in the circus: the rusted Ferris wheel and the silent carousel and the abandoned cotton candy stand.

I run all the way to the end of the winter camp, to the water—the lake where the Giant once caught fish. I stop to drink, drink, drink. I am so thirsty. I drink until I see a winter fish, swimming silver and quick.

The fish startles me; it makes me think too much of Bill. Bill loved to hold a fishing pole in water, waiting patiently for the nibbling bites of hungry fish. I wish he were with me still.

I begin to run again. My ears flap; my trunk swings; my feet pound the ground. I sound powerful. Cars stop on the road and people use their phones to take my picture. Somebody screams.

"An elephant! It could kill us! Get back in the car!"

I would not kill anything. I have never hurt anyone.

The Alligator Boy

I am out of breath, wheezing a little bit, running with this unusual-looking boy who joined me just past Grandma's trailer. He is apparently one of the neighbors, and it must be that boy they told me about.

The kid has this weird skin condition. He's all wrinkled, like an alligator except more rumpled in a human flesh kind of way. He has pitch-black long and floppy skater hair, and he's wearing a faded Led Zeppelin T-shirt, which I guess kind of goes well with old-man skin.

"Queenie Grace, she'll run toward the lake," the boy says, panting. "I saw her take off."

Luckily, there isn't much time for me to stare, or to ask any questions. We're actually way too busy running to be awkward. You don't have much time to be shy when you're on the trail (or tail) of a runaway elephant.

We run and run, quiet except for our shoes and our breath, through the trailer park with its glitzy Christmas decorations. Nothing more disorienting than Santa and reindeer and gigantic inflatable snowmen when it's sunny and seventy-five degrees.

I'm wheezing worse, with that tight-chest feeling I sometimes get. My heart is a crazy thing, and it's like invisible fingers are choking my throat. The boy is breathing hard, too. We run in pretty much the same rhythm, as if we've practiced, slapping the baking macadam as we run around potholes and big jagged stones.

"Watch that hole," the kid gasps, and I swerve around a big dip that might go clear to China. A few people stare, but I don't care. Nobody knows me here.

"Hey, Henry Jack!" croaks an old man, but we just keep going.

We pound out of the trailer park, past the giant boot statue, and now we are running on the real road: yellow lines and blue sky and signs. Plus cars. Dad would have a conniption if he knew this.

"There she is!" huffs the boy, and we both skid to a stop by the side of the road.

Queenie Grace looms between green trees just off the right side of the road, drinking from a lake. Cars are stopping, and shocked people are going wild with surprise. All I see are cell phones, held up, clicking pictures. All I hear are voices, saying the same thing: "Elephant!"

Queenie Grace stops drinking, swings her head for a glimpse of the road, and then starts to run. I can feel the thunder of her weight shaking the earth from here. We'll never catch her. She's a wild animal and she's going to go where she wants to go, do what she wants to do. Run if she wants to run.

"Queenie Grace!" calls the boy. "Wait. Please stop! Wait for us!"

She does. The elephant stops in her tracks, remains frozen in place.

"I . . . can't . . . believe . . . she . . . listened," I say, panting, bending forward and trying to catch my breath. I look up at the boy beside me.

The boy smiles, which is quite a sight when his face is a human map of crinkles and ruts in his skin. It's as if his entire face turns into a crumpled-up piece of paper that some little kid scribbled on.

"This elephant always listens to me," the boy says. "We're like that." He crosses his middle finger over his index finger in that way of wishing for something lucky.

We take off again, but not nearly as fast, and when we finally arrive by the side of the patiently waiting elephant, we stop again to catch our breath. Queenie Grace just stands there, like this is any old normal day, and without thinking,

I lay my hand against her. She is warm, almost like an enormous friendly dog. I leave my hand there for a few seconds, letting it sink in: *I am touching an elephant. My. Hand. Is. On. The. Elephant.*

"She stopped because she totally knows me," says the boy. He leans his forehead against the elephant for a few seconds, as if he's pressing away a headache. Or maybe he's just extremely relieved.

"Wonder why she ran away," he says. "She never does that."

"Well, they chained her up to this tree last night," I reply. "She broke a window and she stole my peanuts and cut her trunk. See, she has a bandage? Then this morning, while we were opening presents, all you heard was her crying and throwing fits. By the time it was dinner, she just broke loose, I guess."

"Wow," says the boy. "They *chained* her? They never chain her!"

I shrug. "Maybe she deserved it. Like being grounded. She was bad, you know. Like now they have to fix the window and all."

The kid shakes his head.

"Queenie Grace is awesome," he says, turning his head to look at me. "She's *always* awesome. We're best friends, Queenie Grace and me. We've known each other since we—*I*—was born. Queenie Grace used to rock my cradle with her trunk."

"I was afraid of her when I was a baby. Actually, I still am."

"You might as well be afraid of the sky," says the boy. "It's way more likely that you'd get hurt by the sky than get hurt by Queenie Grace."

The kid's skin is as wrinkled as the elephant's, and he's quite comfortable keeping his cheek pressed against her side. The elephant swings her head to look back at him and she almost seems to smile, then she reaches her trunk over and hugs his shoulders with it. It's a surprising moment, and I melt a little bit inside, kind of like when you're watching a movie with a sweet scene and the background music tells you to feel the feelings.

"I've known this elephant all my life," says the boy. "More than twelve years. By the way, my name's Henry Jack. Henry Jack O'Toole, otherwise known as the Alligator Boy. I was part of the Twins with Alligator Skin, but now it's just me."

"So where is the other one?"

"He died," says Henry Jack O'Toole, all matter-of-fact. "Sometimes people with this condition don't live too long."

"Oh." I never know what to say to something like that.

"See, when you work with the circus, they like to make a big deal about skin," Henry Jack says. He steps back from

Queenie Grace and flips his hair away from his face by throwing his head back like a rock star.

"Like there's Elephant Skin and Rubber Skin and Elastic Skin and Armadillo Skin and Butterfly Skin. But really, skin is just skin. It comes in different colors, and random states of wrinkled-ness, but really it's all the same. It just covers what's underneath, the important stuff, the organs and the bones and the heart and the soul."

I nod, look down at the elephant's monstrous feet, take a few steps back. It's so quiet here by the water, under the trees, that I can almost hear her tail swishing back and forth, and I definitely hear elephant breath. Sometimes it sounds like snoring. Plus my own whistling-wheezing breathing. Not that I need my inhaler, not yet.

"So you're Lily, right?" asks Henry Jack. "Lily Rose. I remember seeing you with Bill, in West Virginia."

"Yes. I'm Lily Pruitt. Bill was my grandpa."

"I know. I'm really sorry about him. About your grandpa."

"Thanks," I say.

"And, oh yeah! You rode Queenie Grace into the big top in West Virginia! I remember she was running like crazy!"

"I'm never doing that again," I say. "I did it for my grandpa."

"I remember him talking about you," says Henry Jack. "He always called you 'Lily Rose.' And he talked about you, like, all the time. Bill bragged about you nonstop."

"Really?"

"Sure." Henry Jack pulls his T-shirt away from his body, fanning himself, and I catch a glimpse of wrinkled belly skin.

"What did he say?"

"Just stuff about how wonderful his perfect granddaughter is, all that."

"Huh," I say. "Well, I'm far from perfect, but maybe he really thought that I was. He is—*was*—so nice."

"I know. Bill was so freaking cool. I could not even believe it when I heard. I still can't."

"I know, right?"

We're so caught up in our conversation that I realize I'm kind of forgetting about the elephant, and the fact that the three of us are in this together. So I stretch my arm out and touch her again, carefully, two fingers, just to remind myself that she is here. That she is real.

Queenie Grace just stands there, patient, swaying her trunk and shifting her weight from side to side. Through the trees, I can see that a few cars remain stopped along the road; people must still be gawking.

"Well, I guess we'd better get this runaway elephant back home," I say. "Before people call the police or shoot at her or something."

"If anybody shoots at Queenie Grace," says Henry Jack, "they are going to have to get through me first. I would take a bullet for this girl."

"Seriously?" I say. "That's cool. Well, not that you would

be shot . . . but that you can love an elephant so much."

Henry Jack O'Toole pats the elephant, looks up into her right eye, and talks soft and low.

"Come on, sweetheart," he says. "We're taking you home."

And Maybe That Is Why Queenie Grace Ran Away

I love the Alligator Boy. I've known him since he was born, since he and his twin were sweet-smelling babies in a double wooden cradle. I liked Henry Jack the best. He cried the least. (He looked up at me and he cooed and he reached out his tiny hands.)

Some people might say that an elephant should not be allowed near newborn babies, but those who live in Gibtown know me. They know that I'm safe to be around babies. I can be trusted with people of any age.

I pretended that Henry Jack was my baby, that he was Little Gray, and that I had my baby every day. His skin looked like my skin. Sometimes if you try hard enough, you can substitute one love for another. I didn't even have to try. I just loved the Alligator Boy.

I follow Henry Jack and Lily. I move toward home.

"Here we are, girl," says Henry Jack. "Home, sweet home."

I hope and pray that there will be no more chains. I pray without getting down on my knees.

No chains, I pray, again, as Lily goes inside to get Violet and Trullia.

Violet comes outside, eyes wild, hair in a frizz, pale skin.

"Queenie Grace!" she calls. "What are we going to do with you?"

I hang my head low, and I moan. The Alligator Boy and the girl Lily both say, "Awww." They understand me.

"I know," says Violet. "I'm sad, too, and when we're sad, sometimes we do things we wouldn't normally consider. I forgive you, Queenie Grace, but please . . . no more breaking windows or running away. Okay? Deal?"

I raise my head, look Violet in the eye, and try to smile. I do my best.

Violet does the same: tries to smile. But in her eyes, I see the same thing that is inside of me: grief. She looks like grief and she smells of grief, and we are bound together by this one terrible thing: missing Bill.

Grief is even worse than chains. It holds you to one place.

And maybe that is why I ran away.

The Care and Feeding of Elephants

Henry Jack and I stand, arms crossed, both of us panting and sweating, watching Mike carry the heavy, clinking chains to Queenie Grace. Now I'm sorry that we brought her back. If I was brave enough to say it, I'd tell Mike to stop. To just stop and let her be. Leave Queenie Grace alone; let her be free.

"She broke that other chain," Mike says to nobody in particular. "Needs heavier ones."

Henry Jack nudges me with his elbow.

"Mike needs to be chained," he says under his breath.

I snicker.

Surprisingly, I might be starting to like this elephant. Maybe just a tiny little bit. Something about the way her eyes shine in the sunlight, and the way she gazes at Henry Jack. I'm pretty sure I saw love in Queenie Grace's eyes when she exchanged looks with the Alligator Boy.

"Mike better not get the *thotti*," mutters Henry Jack.

"The hottie?"

"*Thotti*," Henry Jack replies. "It's like a Hindu word for 'hook.'"

"Why would Mike get a hook?"

"To punish Queenie Grace," Henry Jack says. "It's what some *mahouts* use to control their elephants."

"*Mahouts*?"

"The guys who ride and train the elephants. It's Hindi, too. You never heard of a *mahout*?"

I shake my head. I'm wheezing, so I sink down into the warm grass. Henry Jack plops next to me. Mike circles the elephant's leg with the chains, hitching her to the tree once again.

"Your grandpa Bill was Queenie Grace's *mahout*," explains Henry Jack. "It's always a boy, usually a kid who gets the elephant when he is little, in other countries. They grow up together, the kid and the elephant, and they get super bonded."

"My grandpa wasn't a little kid when he got Queenie Grace," I say. "He was already married. I think it was before my mother was even born. Yeah, it was. My mother is only thirty. She had me when she was just eighteen."

"The age of the *mahout* isn't the important thing," says Henry Jack. "What matters is the bond. And your grandpa sure was bonded with Queenie Grace. It's like their hearts were superglued."

I lean back on my elbows. The Florida sunshine does feel good, that's for sure. Now I can understand those tourist brochures. Any place that feels this good in wintertime is all right with me.

Queenie Grace uses her trunk to throw some dust into the air. I sneeze.

"She's just covering herself with dust so she doesn't get sunburned," Henry Jack says. "That's what elephants do."

"How do you know so much?" I ask. "You're like an elephant expert."

Henry Jack grins.

"Well, I grew up with them," he says. "Plus, I read a lot. My favorite book is actually this old book that your grandpa gave me. It's called *Manual for Mahouts: The Care and Feeding of Elephants*. I also collect books about sideshows and circus freaks and all that."

"Cool," I say.

Henry Jack shrugs.

"Yeah, sure," he says. "Whatever. Not so cool when you have ichthyosis, though."

"Ick what?"

"Ichthyosis: this skin condition that I have. It just basically means that I have super-dry skin, and it keeps flaking off and getting really scaly. In circuses, like I was telling you, it's usually called 'alligator skin,' or sometimes 'elephant skin.' Nobody really knows how it happens or how to make it not happen. It's just one of those things you have to deal with. Or rather, *I* have to deal with."

I look at Queenie Grace, who's throwing a big hissy fit about the chain. Dust flies; the elephant kicks.

Grandma Violet blusters out of the house like a small and sudden storm.

"Mike!" she yells. "I told you not to chain her!"

"I'm doing it for her own good," Mike shouts back. He has a lit cigarette in his mouth, and some ashes drop to the ground. "For *our* own good."

The fire-eater next door is looking out his window. Those annoying dogs are yipping again, their high yaps straining through the screen.

"Chain it!" the man barks. "I don't want that thing running loose! It's dangerous!"

"*He's* dangerous," Henry Jack mutters. "Somebody needs to chain Charlie."

I can smell heavy cigar smoke from the fire-eater, plus Mike's smoke. I take a big breath, puff out my cheeks, and blow. There's tension in the air, and it's building. I'm pretty good at sensing tension.

Grandma Violet catches up to Mike, and she shoves his shoulder. She kneels down and yanks away at the chains, a furious and determined look on her face.

"Bill would never stand for this!" she snaps. "Never!"

Mike takes a step back, strokes his chin. He watches my grandma, all hunched over, undoing the chains. A sneer is on his face, disdain for my grandma and the elephant. Then Mike moves closer to the back side of Queenie Grace, and glances down at my grandma. He takes the cigarette from his mouth, pinches it between his fingers. Mike sneakily reaches out his hand, cigarette held low, blows smoke.

Henry Jack sits up quickly. "Holy showman," he says. "Did you see that? Did you see what just happened?"

"It looked like he touched the cigarette to the elephant's skin," I whisper. "Like he burned her on purpose."

"Are you sure?" Henry Jack asks. "Would you swear on your life?"

"No," I said. "Are you?"

"I'm not one hundred percent sure," he says. "But that's what it looked like."

"I know."

"I swear," murmurs Henry Jack, gritting his teeth. "If that guy hurt Queenie Grace, I'm going to lose it. He's going to get a piece of me . . . and this fist."

Henry Jack raises a clenched, wrinkled fist, shaking it in the air, fixing eyes of steel on Mike.

"I never did like that guy," he says. "There's something fishy about him."

"And that's no way to treat an elephant," I reply. Even I know that.

Henry Jack and I fix eye daggers on creepy Mike. He puts the cigarette back in his mouth and puffs away. Queenie Grace quakes and shakes.

Queenie Grace Feels Fire

I am burned. The man Mike did this once before with his cigarette, but nobody noticed. Not even Bill, because sly Mike did it on my underside.

I feel the spot on my back, seared, sore. I feel fire.

This man Mike is full of anger. He is full of anger and he is full of danger and he is full of hate.

I can smell it from a mile away.

Nobody Deserves to Be Hurt, Not Even an Elephant

Grandma Violet has set Queenie Grace free.

"Now go put away those chains," she says to Mike. She is breathing hard, chest heaving. I hope she doesn't have a heart attack, too.

"Put them away now, and I never want to see them again," Grandma says.

Mike picks up the chains, slinks into the little pink shed. We can hear the throwing-down clinking sounds from here. If metal has the ability to sound angry, it's doing it now.

My grandma is still ferocious, fuming, lips a thin line and her brow furrowed. My tiny grandma brims full of old-lady fury. She has her own personal storm cloud hanging over her head.

"Should we tell her?" I ask Henry Jack. "About what Mike did?"

He shakes his head.

"Not yet. Let her calm down first; we'll check it out. No use getting her all worked up if it didn't even happen."

Grandma stomps inside, and I swear you can see fire flaming from her eyes. Queenie Grace just stands there, trunk swaying, as if she's feeling awkward about the whole mess.

"I can hear you breathing," Henry Jack says. "Wheezing."

"It's from the running," I explain. "My asthma kicks up when I run. Or when I get super tired. Or upset. Or stressed."

I pull my ever-present inhaler from my pocket, take a puff. Hold it in; blow it out.

"There. All better. No more whistle."

"I wish everything was that simple to fix."

"Oh, it's not always that simple. A couple of times, when it was bad, I actually had to go to the ER. This one time, I had to stay overnight. And wear a hospital gown, and get an IV."

"That stinks," says Henry Jack. "I've been in the hospital, too. Can't stand that place."

I shrug. "That's life."

Mike skulks inside, and Henry Jack and I decide it's time to check out Queenie Grace. Or at least, Henry Jack will check her out. I'm not getting that close, not yet.

I stay back a couple of cautious yards and watch as Henry Jack leans in to peer closely at the elephant's skin. He reaches out with his index finger and grazes it, and I can tell from here that the touch is barely there, so gentle.

He looks back at me and shakes his head, biting his lip, and then he nods.

"Yep," he says. "It's a burn, all right. Little circle, like the tip of a cigarette."

Henry Jack strides back to me, and I can tell he's bubbling over with hot fury, too. He makes a fist with one hand and punches the open palm of his other hand.

"Bam," he says. "That guy Mike . . ."

"How could somebody do that?"

"People do the craziest things," says Henry Jack. "Humans are actually worse than animals."

"What are we going to do?" I ask. "Shouldn't we tell my grandma?"

"I think we should wait," says Henry Jack. "Right after somebody dies isn't a great time to hear bad news like that. I'm worried that Violet's feeling too stressed, and this would be just one more thing."

"Yeah," I agreed, "she is really stressed. I'm kind of scared that she might have a heart attack, like my grandpa did."

"That actually occurred to me, too."

"So, then what are we going to do?"

"Come with me to my place," Henry Jack replies. "I need

that *mahout* book I told you about. I don't know how to treat a burn, but we'll find out."

"And what are we going to do about Mike?" I ask as we hurry together across the yards. The three little dogs are yipping again, and it's getting hotter by the minute. I have to keep reminding myself that this is Christmas Day. That's way strange, when you forget a holiday because you're in a place with people who just don't feel like celebrating.

"I don't even know what to say about Mike," Henry Jack replies. "He's a dirtbag. And I'm not sure what to do about dirtbags. We need to figure out a plan to get rid of him, I guess."

"Don't you have a book about that?" I ask.

We both laugh, and that's how I know we're becoming good friends, because that combo laugh says without words, *I get it. We're in this together.*

Henry Jack's trailer is a nice double-wide, with lots of colorful pictures on the wood-paneled walls. It smells shiny and clean, like somebody was just super-housecleaning with lots of Pine-Sol and Pledge and Windex. The air conditioner hums; it feels great in here.

"I like your house," I say.

"It's a home," Henry Jack replies. "Just me and my mom, but we fill it up just right. My favorite time is December, when we get to stay here in one place. All. Month. Long. All the other months, we travel in a motor home, just like your grandparents do. Did."

"Is your mom in the circus, too?"

"Yeah, she's a girl on the flying trapeze," he says. "Just like your mom."

"Trullia. You can call her Trullia; I do."

A lady floats gracefully out of one of the rooms. She's pretty: hair like black licorice, shimmery dark eyes, tanned skin. She's thin, yet strong-looking, with muscles in her arms and legs.

"Hi!" she says. "You must be Lily. Bill's granddaughter. I'm Faith, Henry Jack's mom. I am so sorry about your grandpa, honey. We were all so fond of him."

"Me too," I say.

Faith walks, or rather *glides*, down the hall. Her walk is like flying: all graceful and smooth, as if she doesn't even have feet.

"Nice to meet you," she says. "Bill always talked about you, how much he adored you and wished he could see you more often."

I nod, feeling awkward.

"So what's up?" asks Faith. She reaches out to Henry Jack and pushes back a bunch of his floppy black hair, and then she lets her fingers rest on his head for a few seconds. It's as if she can hardly let go of him. I wish I had a mom like that.

"Well, we just need to check something out in one of my

books," replies Henry Jack. "Plus get my sunburn stuff."

"Okay," she says. "And be sure not to get sunburned, sweetie. Lily, you are in my prayers."

"Thank you," I say. I think it's an honor to be in somebody's prayers.

Faith floats off down the hallway, and I follow Henry Jack into his bedroom. The walls are covered with posters from old circus sideshows, and there are bunk beds.

"Why do you have a bunk bed?" I ask. "Are there two of you?" Right after I say it, I get this sinking feeling, remembering what he'd said about his brother.

"Used to be," Henry Jack replies. "Remember I told you: I was one of the Twins with Alligator Skin. Well, I really was a twin. I had a brother, identical, one minute older than me. His name was Jeremy Zack, and he died when we were eleven."

"I'm sorry. I never knew anybody who lost a brother."

"It's okay," says Henry Jack. "He was really sick a lot, in pain, all that. So I know he's in a better place, like they say."

"Are you sick a lot and in pain, too?"

"Only if I get sunburned," Henry Jack says. "The sun is my worst enemy."

"That's sad," I say. "Sunshine is usually such a happy thing."

Henry Jack shrugs.

"I used to be mad about everything. Like, I was ticked off about our dad, our disease, Mom having to work so hard all the time. But then something happened that made me change."

"What happened?" I ask.

Henry Jack looks down, as if he's closing his eyes, clenching his teeth, and reaching deep into a scary memory.

"Jeremy Zack got sick," he says. "Really sick. Like his skin got worse and worse and worse, until there was hardly anything left of him, almost nothing left to protect him from the world. It actually felt like I was looking at a ghost: the ghost of my brother."

"And that didn't make you even madder?"

"Yeah, at first," says Henry Jack. "I was mad at the world. But one day, Jeremy Zack said seven words that changed everything. He said, 'You're only hurting yourself. Get over it.'"

Henry Jack swallows hard. He looks up at me.

"Those were some of his last words, right before he died."

"Wow." I don't know what else to say.

"Yeah. So those words, they changed everything. All of a sudden, I started seeing the good side of things. And believe it or not, *everything*—even bad stuff—has something good included; it really does. I play this little game with myself when I try to find the good things. I call it 'the bright side.' Want me to teach you how to play?"

"Sure."

"Okay. Give me something bad. Something you don't like in your life."

"Ummm . . . my mom left."

"The good: You got even closer to your dad," says Henry Jack. "Give me another one."

"I have asthma."

"The good: You learned to appreciate breathing. Not everybody does, you know. Give me another."

"I . . . have weird hair."

"The good: Your hair makes you unique. Not many people have pure red hair, you know. Like, maybe you could even get a part in some movie, playing the part of an Irish girl. And then next thing you know, you might be filming in Ireland! Getting paid for it! Seeing a cool new place, and all because of that red hair you hate. See how it works?"

"Yeah," I say. "I guess."

"The bright side is always there," says Henry Jack. "Even when it's hiding, it's still there. Like my bright side of having this skin condition is that I get to be in the circus."

"So, do you actually *like* working in the circus?" I'm not going to say this to Henry Jack, but it seems to me that it's mean to put a kid with a skin condition in a sideshow. Although his mom seems anything but mean.

"I don't like working in the circus," says Henry Jack. "I *love* working in the circus. It's definitely the bright side of being a freak."

"So it doesn't bother you, being called a . . . *freak*?"

"Nah," says Henry Jack. "It's all just part of the act; goes along with the job. Plus, I do other stuff than just being seen for my skin. Like I do this thing with monkeys that I trained to count."

"Cool. So how long have you been working in the circus?"

"It was our idea—mine and Jeremy Zack's—to be the Twins with Alligator Skin. We were nine years old when we came up with our plan," Henry Jack explains. "Mom didn't really want us to do that, but we were in the mood for something to do, plus we wanted to help make some money."

"Well," I say, "I guess that's a good point. If I could make money with this stupid asthma, I'd go for it."

"Yep," says Henry Jack. "And with me not having a dad, it's good to help Mom with the bills."

"Where's your dad?" I ask.

"Who knows?" says Henry Jack. He shrugs. "Never met him, but that's okay. I have enough dads, anyway, right here in Gibtown. Like your grandpa Bill. He was like a dad to me."

"My grandpa was a lot of things to a lot of people," I say. "He was like five guys in one."

Henry Jack grins. He goes to a shelf filled with books. He pulls one out and holds it like a treasure. It's thick, and red, and the front cover is beaten up like it's been loved.

"Here it is," he says. "This is the book your grandpa gave me."

We both sit on the bottom bunk, hunched over the book, as Henry Jack pages through. A sentence about wounds catches my eye.

"Hey!" I say. "Wait a minute! That says never use hydrogen peroxide on a fresh cut. Well, I'm pretty sure that last night, they used it on Queenie Grace's trunk, after she broke the window to eat my peanuts."

"Jeez," says Henry Jack. "They need to read this book."

He flips through a few more pages and gets to a section about burns.

"Iodine," he says. "We need this stuff called iodine."

"Where can we find that?"

"George's Pharmacy," Henry Jack says. "They have everything."

George's Pharmacy is inside a small brick building just down the street. Shelves of antique medicine bottles line the walls as decoration, and there's an old-fashioned soda fountain. George himself is behind the counter, which comes up to my knees. George is a small man, a very little person.

"Hey, hey," he says in a nasally voice. "Mr. Henry Jack. What can I do for you?"

"We need iodine," replies Henry Jack. "For a little burn on a big elephant."

"Oh, sorry to hear that about my sweetie Queenie Grace," George says, shaking his head, which is covered in sparse and spiky gray hair. "And I still can't believe that Bill's gone. Man, what a shock. Here one minute, gone the next."

"I know," says Henry Jack. "And this is his granddaughter, Lily."

"Well, I'll be! I am so sorry about your grandpa," says George. He reaches up a small and pudgy hand, and I shake it. "You're the spittin' image of your grandma and with your grandpa's height: so tall and willowy, with that long, beautiful hair and eyes shimmery as blueberry Kool-Aid. Plus, you have your mother's cute dimples."

"Um, thanks?" I say.

Henry Jack snickers.

"George here always did have a crush on Miss Violet," he says.

George waves away his words like he's swatting a fly.

"Okay, back to business," he says, slapping his hand on the wooden counter. "So how did Queenie Grace get burned?"

"A bad guy," says Henry Jack.

"Mike? Or Fire-Eatin' Charlie?"

"Wow, good guess," Henry Jack says. "How'd you know?"

"Only two bad guys I can think of. So which one was it?"

"That's for us to know," Henry Jack says, paying for the iodine. "And you to find out."

"And believe me," George states, handing Henry Jack his change, "I will find out. I know most everything that goes on in this town. And whoever hurt that elephant is going to have to answer to me!"

"And me," Henry Jack adds.

I don't want to be left out, so I put in my two cents.

"And me," I say. "Nobody deserves to be hurt. Not even an elephant."

"That's right, darlin'," says George. "You sure do have your grandfather's kindness, I can tell. Now you try to enjoy the holiday, okay?"

I nod.

"And maybe next time I see you two, just maybe, I'll tell you some crazy stories about that guy Mike and Fire-Eatin' Charlie. Not nice stories, but true stories."

"Why not tell us now?" Henry Jack asks.

"It's Christmas," replies George. "Not a day for those stories."

"Aren't most stores closed on Christmas?" I ask, and George shrugs.

"If I closed the store, I'd be alone, except for my poor old lion, Boldo," he says. "This way, I get to see my friends. That's the best way to spend a holiday: seeing people I like. And helping them."

"And helping elephants, too," I say as Henry Jack tucks the bottle of iodine in the pocket of his shorts.

"That's right, girlie. And Mr. Henry Jack: you're looking sorta red. Make sure you don't get sunburned, okay?"

Queenie Grace Doesn't Like Iodine

I don't like iodine. It burns worse than the burn burns.

I flinch, skin quivering. I don't like the iodine, but I do like that the Alligator Boy is taking care of me.

The girl Lily stands far back, watching. She's always watching. She's always standing back, staying away. Sometimes she shakes. I can hear her breath. It's a slight whistle, quieter than the tiger trainer's whistle. The girl has asthma. Bill had asthma, too, when the dust swirled or when he was in a place with summertime flowers.

I wonder if Lily will ever like me. And I wonder if I could maybe one day like the girl.

Probably not. I know that some friendships are just not meant to be.

A Smack in the Face

So I'm getting braver, plus Queenie Grace is shaking a little, so I decide to carefully stand beside her while Henry Jack works. I pat her gently, as he uses the dropper to dribble brownish-orange liquid onto Queenie Grace's cigarette burn. Red blossoms out like a blooming flower on the elephant's rough gray skin.

"It's okay, girl," I whisper. "It's okay."

But the elephant doesn't like the iodine. She flinches and quivers, and then she swings her trunk, hard.

Queenie Grace's trunk slaps my face. It feels like the hand of a boneless giant.

"Owwww!" I holler, holding a hand to my cheek. I sink to my knees in the grass. "She hit me!"

"I don't think she tried to hit you," says Henry Jack.

"I know. But still. It hurts."

I stand up, holding my cheek. Queenie Grace just looks at me. Then I step back, back, back . . . until no part of the elephant can possibly reach me. I'm rubbing my cheek. It smarts, and I'm starting to have a headache, too.

"What's going on? Who the heck was screaming? Can't we have any peace around here, even on Christmas?"

It's Grandma Violet, standing on the little porch and yelling across the yard.

"No worries," Henry Jack calls back. "Just a little accident with an elephant slap. It's fine."

"Yes," I say. "You can go back inside, Grandma. I'm fine."

But my grandma obviously doesn't believe that, because she's already making her way across the yard, past the tree, directly to me. I keep my hand on my cheek.

"Let me see," Grandma Violet commands.

I take away my hand

"Good grief," my grandma says. "There's a huge red mark! I bet that's going to bruise."

I shrug. "It's okay," I say.

"No," says Grandma Violet. "It's not okay."

Trullia comes out, wearing shorts that are way too short and a top that barely covers her belly button.

"What happened?" she asks.

"Queenie Grace accidentally slapped Lily," Grandma says.

Trullia strolls over, tugs down her shirt, plucks down her shorts.

"It doesn't look too bad," she says. "How did it happen?"

"It was an accident," I say. I can't believe that I am actually defending the elephant.

Mike's watching now from the doorway of the trailer, blowing smoke.

"What happened?" he asks.

"It was an accident," says Henry Jack.

Grandma Violet shakes a finger at the elephant, the way a mother lovingly reprimands a little kid.

"Queenie Grace!" she exclaims. "You know better."

"No, she doesn't!" yells Fire-Eating Charlie, who's back outside, smoking a cigar. "It's a wild animal, and it's going to act wild! I keep telling you people."

"Hush, Charlie," Grandma snaps back. "It's none of your business."

"It's my business when that elephant wallops one of my dogs!"

"Your dog was biting her leg!" Grandma shrieks.

"Well, don't worry; it won't happen again," Fire-Eating Charlie shouts. "Because of that elephant, I have to keep my dogs inside! The only time they come out is when they need to go potty."

Henry Jack snickers.

"Go potty," he whispers. "Big tough fire-eating cigar-smoking Charlie and his itsy wittle doggies that wear pink tutus and *go potty*. Plus that ugly beard of his. Did you know that a beard has more germs than a toilet?"

"Ewwwwww," I say. "Thanks for sharing that."

"Charlie's got a point about the danger," Mike calls, in between puffing away. "A wild animal is going to do wild things. It's in their nature."

"Zip it, Mike," Grandma says.

"The thing hurt your granddaughter!" Mike says. "Smacked her right in the face! And you're not going to put it in the chains."

"No," says Grandma Violet. "I'm not. Queenie Grace is obviously not herself, but none of us are quite right at this time. So let it go."

Mike throws down his cigarette and grinds it out with his flip-flop, then throws up his hands.

"I'm going in," he says. "You guys interrupted my TV show."

Trullia is not expressing any opinion. She's now sitting in a lawn chair, smoking, inspecting her legs like a monkey picking bugs.

"Don't know what my daughter sees in that man," Grandma mutters. She's sweating, and she lifts her long hair from her neck with one hand, fanning her face with the other. Grandma Violet is wearing a T-shirt version of the

Ugly Christmas Sweater: all green and red, with a Rudolph and Santa. Rudolph has a red light for his nose, and it blinks: *Off. On. Off. On.*

"I'm sorry, Lily, honey," Grandma says. She pulls me into a hug. "Not a very relaxing visit, is it? I apologize for everything."

"It's okay," I say.

"No," Grandma says, "it's not okay. Poor Grandpa would have hated all this commotion. He would have wanted you to have a nice peaceful Christmas visit."

And then Grandma notices the red blotch on Queenie Grace.

"What is that red spot?" she asks, and Henry Jack looks at me. We both shuffle our feet. I have no idea what to say, and apparently, neither does Henry Jack. The silence is heavy as Grandma bends close to inspect the red spot on Queenie Grace's skin.

"Why, there's a little circle of a burn mark!" Grandma says. "It's the size of a cigarette! Did somebody . . . did Mike . . . *burn* her?" she asks, a look of horror crossing her face.

"Yes," Henry Jack says. "With his cigarette, when you were taking off the chains. We went and got some iodine, put it on the burn. I thought maybe we should wait to tell you. You know, you already have so much on your mind. Plus, we weren't completely one hundred percent sure until now. Not like swear-your-life-on-it certain."

"We were hoping that maybe it was an accident," I add, my voice quiet and trembly.

"This was no accident! That man!" Grandma Violet says. "He's going to have to go. Trullia, get over here!"

Trullia heaves herself up, saunters over.

"Look what your boyfriend did!" Grandma says. She points to the burned spot on Queenie Grace. "With a cigarette, for heaven's sakes! What is wrong with that man?"

Trullia glances at the burn.

"Oh, Mom," she says. "I'm sure it was an accident, and it probably wasn't even Mike."

"It was Mike, all right, and it was on purpose," Henry Jack says. "We saw him. Me and Lily were watching."

Trullia's eyes widen, and confusion covers her face.

"But . . . why?" she says. "Why on earth would he do that? Queenie Grace is so sweet."

"Anybody who would hurt an elephant like that," says Grandma, "has problems. Big problems."

"Well, I told you about his childhood and all that," says Trullia. "He had it rough. Remember, his mother pushed him down the steps? Pulled his hair and stuff? His childhood was tough."

"That is no excuse!" Grandma Violet says. "That man needs to own his mistakes, take responsibility! Why, I have half a mind to call the police on him!"

"Mom," says Trullia. "Please. Give him one more chance."

Grandma just takes a big breath, shakes her head.

"Go tell him," she says, slow and firm. "Tell him to get out of here and never come back. I don't want him in my home."

Trullia stomps off. Henry Jack and I stare at our feet.

"Maybe we shouldn't have told you," he says to Grandma. "It's like, you don't need that on top of . . . everything else."

"Oh, it's good you told me, honey," Grandma says to Henry Jack. "We all need to look out for one another."

Grandma hugs Henry Jack, then me. She leans into Queenie Grace and kisses her skin.

"I'm so sorry," she says to the elephant. "I'm so sorry you've had to deal with him."

Grandma steps back, looks at Henry Jack and me.

"Mike's not happy with himself," she says. "And it comes out against everything and everybody else. Not that it's an excuse. It is what it is."

I nod. This is beginning to sound like a conversation with the school guidance counselor. "How's your face, sweetie?" Grandma asks.

"It's okay. It's fine."

Grandma just looks up at Queenie Grace's face for a few minutes, as her Christmas shirt winks off and on. Queenie Grace looks back, blinking. There's love in her eyes, love in Grandma's eyes, a shared bond between them.

"No more swinging that trunk," Grandma says to the elephant. "Be a good girl."

"She'll be good," Henry Jack says. "Queenie Grace is the best elephant I know."

Trunks Are Very Difficult to Manage

I did not mean to hit the girl Lily in the face. Humans just don't understand: trunks are sometimes very difficult to manage.

My skin is beginning to cool. Violet tells me to be good. I always do my best to be good.

If only Bill were here. An elephant without her *mahout* is nothing.

Sunburn

Grandma goes inside, and there's the sound of yelling. Henry Jack and I act as if it's not happening.

"You look like you have sunburn," I say.

"Shoot," Henry Jack says, studying his arm, then his legs. "I do. My mom is going to kill me, if this sunburn doesn't kill me first."

"Sunburn could kill you?"

"Sure. With this skin condition, I'm supposed to be super careful."

"So why aren't you?"

"I am. It's just that I forgot, in the excitement of actually having somebody to hang out with. Kids our age aren't exactly that common here in Gibtown."

"I noticed."

Henry Jack and I walk quickly back to his house so that he can use his sunburn cream. His mother smells it from down the hall and comes floating into his room.

"Henry. Jack. O'Toole," she says, his name all spaced out like seeds in a garden. "You. Are. Sunburned."

"I know," says Henry Jack. "Not that bad, actually. Don't worry, Mom. I'm taking care of it."

Faith holds a hand to her heart.

"I swear, you give me a heart attack sometimes," she says. But then she remembers about my grandpa having a heart attack, because her face scrunches and she changes the subject.

"So, Lily," Faith says. "Did you inherit your mother's talent for the flying trapeze?"

"I . . . don't think so," I reply. "I'm scared of heights."

"Have you ever tried?"

"Um, no. It's not like there's lots of opportunity for that in West Virginia."

Faith laughs. She tosses back her long black hair and lifts her arms, pretending to be flying on a trapeze.

"One day while you're here," she says, "I will teach you. I'll teach you to fly."

Henry Jack slathers himself with more smelly lotion, and he promises to stay inside for the rest of daylight hours. We both sit on the top bunk this time, heads grazing the ceiling. It's weird to think that his brother slept here.

"How's your asthma?" Henry Jack asks, and I shrug.

"Good. Normal. How's your sunburn?"

"Bad. Normal. So do you want to play a game or something?" Henry Jack asks. "We could play video games. Or this game called Apples to Apples that I got for Christmas. Or cards."

"No, thanks," I reply. "I guess I'd better get back to my grandma's. See if Trullia got rid of Mike."

"Why do you call her Trullia?"

"That's her name."

"But she's your mom."

"Yeah, but no. Not really. She left, like when I was three. My dad raised me. I only see her every now and then."

"So why'd she leave?"

"Beats me. I'm still trying to figure that out. We live in this awesome place called Magic Mountain, a campground, with a swimming pool and mini-golf and hiking trails. It's a great place, at least in the summer, when all the flowers are blooming and we can be outside. Winter's not so good."

"Sounds like you're pretty lucky," Henry Jack says. "You get to go to school, a regular school. If you were like me, on the road, you'd have to mostly learn on your own, plus have a tutor."

I shrug. "Yeah," I say. "I guess."

"It must feel weird, though," he says. "Not to have your mom."

"It does. I used to actually pretend she was dead, because I thought that was better than knowing she just didn't want to stay with us."

Henry Jack's quiet for a minute.

"At least I have a great dad," I say, looking for the bright side. "And our campground. And my painting. I love to paint, more than just about anything. That's one thing that Queenie Grace and I have in common: painting. Actually, it might be the only thing we have in common. Grandpa taught both of us to paint."

"Speaking of Queenie Grace," says Henry Jack. "See that picture hanging over there?"

He points to a painting with slashes of blue and green and purple and red.

"Queenie Grace painted that!" he says. "Me and Jeremy Zack stood together and we asked her to paint us, and that's what she painted."

"Cool."

"I think I'm the blue and green," says Henry Jack. "He was more fiery and hyper, so he must have been the purple and red."

Just then my cell phone beeps with a text.

"It's from my grandma," I say. "I didn't even know she knew how to text."

"She wears Chuck Taylor sneakers and has purple hair," says Henry Jack. "She knows how to text."

I kicked Mike out, says the text. He won't be here when you get back.

"She kicked him out," I say. "She got rid of Mike."

"Good," says Henry Jack. "I hope he doesn't show up at the funeral."

My stomach drops.

"What's wrong?" asks Henry Jack. He flips back his hair, peering at me.

"The funeral," I say. "I've never been to one."

"There's a bright side to funerals, too," he says. "You get to say good-bye. Look at their face one last time."

I sigh. "I'm nervous."

"Don't worry," says my new friend, and his voice is like a warm, fuzzy blanket thrown over me when I'm cold. "I'll be there for you."

And I know that he will.

Queenie Grace Feels Pain for Henry Jack

My burn is feeling a little bit better, after just one day. My trunk is also healing. My back is healing. The only thing that is not healing is my heart. It is still broken, missing Bill. But I'm trying to enjoy the Tuesday morning sunshine, watching the girl Lily paint a picture of the Alligator Boy.

Except in this picture, Henry Jack does not have alligator skin. He does not have elephant skin.

Henry Jack has the skin of a normal boy in Lily's painting. He sits in a lawn chair in the yard, smiling, staring into the distance as she paints away.

I wish Henry Jack did not have his wrinkled skin. I know that it gives him pain. He is in pain today, with red color from the sun on his face.

I feel pain for Henry Jack. He feels pain for me. That is what best friends do.

Painting Is Almost Magic

It's the day after Christmas, and I'm just finishing up the painting of Henry Jack when George stops by.

"Wow," says George in his high, nasally voice. He's wearing a beret and he tips it, studying my painting with his head tilted back.

"Wow," he says again. "That's really good, Miss Lily. You're very talented."

"Thanks. I've been painting all my life."

"Maybe I could pay you to paint me. Me and Boldo, my lion!"

I bite my lip.

"I'm . . . kind of scared of lions," I say.

"Oh, Boldo's a big pussycat!" George says. "He wouldn't hurt you, I promise. When my grandkids come to visit, they play with him as if he's just a huge overgrown kitty."

I shrug.

"Okay," I say. "I could do that." I'm trying to conquer my fears.

Queenie Grace is standing in the shade of the nearby tree, and George waves at her.

"Hello, sweetie," he says.

I swear her lips curl into a smile and she raises her trunk. Queenie Grace walks with those huge feet, lifting them delicately like an enormous clumsy ballerina, in our direction.

"Lily here is just like you," George says to the elephant. "A talented artist. I have a bunch of Queenie Grace's paintings hanging in my place. She's famous in the elephant art world."

"Obvious that we're related then, huh?" I ask, and George laughs.

"Yep," he says. "Something very similar in those eyes." He looks from side to side, checking out my eyes and then the elephant's.

Henry Jack and I laugh.

"And the cool thing is that my grandpa taught us both to paint," I say. "He taught me, and he taught Queenie Grace."

"Bill lives on," Henry Jack says, "in your paintings. Yours and Queenie Grace's."

"You're looking extra red today," George says to Henry Jack. "You been using your sunburn cream?"

"Yes, Mom," Henry Jack says, rolling his eyes. "I swear,

you're as bad as her."

"But not nearly as pretty!" jokes George, and we laugh again. Even Queenie Grace seems to chuckle, in that snoring snuffling kind of way.

"So I wanted to check out the cigarette burn," George says, and Henry Jack points.

"Right back there," he says. "You can't miss it. And it was definitely him. It was Mike."

"Do you have a step stool?" asks George. "Or a ladder?"

Henry Jack stands up from the lawn chair, stretches, and then he just lifts George up, hands circling George's pudgy waist. George inspects the red circle on Queenie Grace's skin.

"What a jerk," he mutters.

"I know," Henry Jack says, lowering George to the ground. "He's staying with Charlie the fire-eater now. Violet kicked him out."

George glares in the direction of the fire-eater's house.

"Neither one of those guys is worth anything," he grumbles. "They deserve each other."

Just then, Henry Jack notices my painting. He stops dead, steps closer, stares at the picture, takes another couple of steps. He reaches out to touch the edge of the canvas, gently, eyes fixed on my painting of him. He looks as if he's seen a ghost.

"Holy showman," he says quietly. "So that's what I'd look

like, if I was just a normal boy."

"Well, you are a normal boy," I say. "But that's just you without the wrinkles. That's all."

Henry Jack looks at me, and his eyes fill with tears.

"Thanks," he says. "I always wanted to see that."

"No wonder Bill bragged so much about you, Lily," says George. "You're one amazing girl."

I toe the ground with my shoe. I'm not used to so many compliments coming at me from all directions.

"Thanks," I say.

"Have you ever painted your grandpa?" asks Henry Jack. "If you haven't, you should."

"I haven't," I say. "But that's a good idea. I'll paint Grandpa Bill."

So the rest of the day and into the night, I paint. I don't paint from a picture; I just paint from memory. I know my grandfather by heart: every line, every smile, every tuft of fluffy white hair. Blue eyes, thin slant of nose, lips that never knew how to frown. White stubble scruffy on his cheeks, a black mole over his straggly left eyebrow. A small slice of scar on his chin, the tiny pit on the right side of his nose where he once had skin cancer.

And when it's finished, it's Grandpa Bill. Grandpa Bill on paper, in paint, come to life once again by the love in my hand.

Grandma comes into the bedroom, wearing her baggy yellow SpongeBob nightshirt, just as I'm finishing.

"Oh," she says, stopping. "Oh, Lily. It's perfect. It's him. Scars and all."

I step back, squint.

"It's him, kind of. But not really. Because he can never really be here again," I say.

Grandma pulls me into a hug.

"He's here," she says. "I can feel him. It's like magic."

And then I realize why I like to paint. It *is* exactly like magic: taking something blank and empty and filling that space *abracadabra* with color and life and light. I want to explain all this to Grandma, the wonder of it all, but I can't find the right words. There are some things in life that just don't fit within twenty-six letters of the alphabet.

"Thanks for the paints," I say.

Queenie Grace Would Never Hurt the People She Loves

I can't stop looking through the living room window at the new painting. The girl Lily painted my *mahout*!

It is morning, Wednesday, and the eastern sun shines a spotlight on the painting. It is like a circus spotlight: a circle of light just like those we stood inside for so many years. We made people smile, Bill and I. We made them cheer.

I go down on my knees, in order to better see inside the trailer.

The mean fire-eater Charlie is outside in his yard.

"Yeah, you'd better pray," he says to me. I smell the cigar; I see the cowboy hat. "You'd better pray that they don't get rid of you soon. Look at you: can't keep away from their house. Next thing ya know, you'll be bustin' out another window and hurtin' somebody."

Charlie is wrong.

I would never hurt people I love.

An Agreement

Two days after Christmas. I've been here in Gibtown since Sunday night, but it feels like a miniature forever. Like a tiny lifetime.

Trullia comes yawning and stretching out of the bathroom as Grandma and I are eating breakfast. She's wearing a trapeze costume, so I guess she plans to practice today, or work, or whatever it is that she does in those clothes.

"Did you notice something different in the living room?" Grandma Violet asks as my mother pads barefoot into the kitchen and pours a cup of coffee.

"Um . . . there's no Mike sleeping there?" Trullia sips her coffee. Her hair streams wet down her back, dripping drops of water on the glittery gold costume.

"No. I don't even want to hear that name! Guess again,"

Grandma says. "Hint: It's something on the wall."

I try not to smile. She's talking about my painting, the portrait of Grandpa. She already put up a hook and hung the unframed canvas on the living room wall.

"Uh . . . you bought an Elf on the Shelf?" Trullia guesses.

"Don't be silly!" Grandma says, laughing. "Look! The wall over the sofa!"

My mother's eyes roam the wall until they land on my painting. She puts down her coffee, not taking her eyes from the portrait, and goes into the living room as if a magnet is pulling her.

"Wow," says Trullia. "This is good. Where'd you have it done?"

"Lily painted it," Grandma says. "Last night, while you were gone."

"Wow," Trullia says again. She looks at me as if I'm somebody she doesn't know, which actually I suppose I am. "You're an awesome artist, Lily," she says. "It looks just like him. It's almost like you brought him back to life."

I shrug.

"I tried," I say. "I know his face by heart."

I'm hoping for more of a conversation about my painting, about my grandpa, about how proud my mother might be of my talent for art. But no. It's not going to happen, because Trullia is hustling back to the kitchen and slurping her coffee.

"I have to hurry," she says, "I'm teaching at trapeze school today, for Faith."

"Maybe you could take Lily," Grandma suggests. "I don't think she has any plans."

I sigh.

"Not exactly," I say. "Maybe just hanging with that kid Henry Jack."

"Well, Mom, it sounds as if she has plans," Trullia says. "I'll see you later today."

And then my mother bangs out through the door, juggling her coffee cup and her purse, an unlit cigarette dangling from her lips. She just leaves me behind, once again, not even looking back before she goes.

My phone beeps. It's a text from my dad.

Everything going OK?

Yes, I text. Fine.

Now that I'm in the painting mood, I want to keep on going. I set up my new easel and canvas outside, in the yard, planning to paint a Florida landscape in shades of yellow and blue and green and orange.

Grandma's on the phone inside, talking about funeral details. I can hear her voice through the screen window, plus the TV sounds of a morning talk show.

Queenie Grace is standing nearby. She keeps staring over at Charlie's place, even though there's nobody outside.

Maybe she can smell Mike. I must be getting to know the elephant, because I can tell that she's nervous. She trembles a little bit when she looks over there, plus she keeps shuffling her feet and rocking. Her eyes swim with fear.

"It's okay, Queenie Grace," I say. "We won't let him hurt you again. He's not coming back here. Don't worry."

Queenie Grace seems to understand. Her eyes shine with something like gratitude, and she walks slowly to my side. I have a bunch of paintbrushes, a cup, and the new paints from Grandma.

I dab a brush in the blue, paint sky. Orange, yellow. Lots of flowers, green grass, and trees.

And then Queenie Grace reaches over with her trunk. She picks up a brush and dunks it in the cup. Water splashes. I laugh, surprised. The elephant dips the brush in the purple paint and adds a swath of color to my sky.

"Good job!" I say. "You're a good painter, Queenie Grace!"

The elephant is standing right next to me, and I'm not even scared, not really. We paint together for a few minutes, and it feels comfortable, as if we've been doing this forever. Her trunk brushes against my arm a few times, but I don't even flinch. Something about putting paint to canvas is so relaxing, and I'm happy. I'm glad that the elephant and I are starting to become friends. I'm getting over my fear. This might be a miracle, a Christmas miracle. Everything feels peaceful, both inside of me and outside.

But then I see something that makes me afraid and gives me the shivers. It's Mike, slinking around in Charlie's yard. He's carrying a tool of some kind, long and sharp, and he looks away when he sees me.

I shudder. Something is just not right about Mike.

Queenie Grace feels it, too.

"Don't worry," I say again, reaching over and patting the elephant. "He won't hurt you anymore. I promise. I swear, I'll do my best to protect you. Hopefully, you'll protect me, too. Deal?"

Queenie Grace pats my arm gently with her trunk. It's an agreement.

Queenie Grace
Paints with Lily

We paint together, the girl and me. I have never before painted with a human, except for when I was taught to paint by Bill.

This feels nice: standing side by side with Lily. I think that perhaps we are becoming friends. Perhaps she is starting to be not so afraid.

But then I feel her shiver. It is Mike. He is in the yard next door. Mike sends knives with his eyes.

I am not worried. I have Lily by my side. And we have promised, we have sworn, to do everything we can to protect each other.

This is what friends do.

Night

I paint most of the day with Queenie Grace, and then Henry Jack shows up as the sun is setting.

"Hey!" he says. "Nice painting! Pretty cool that you two are hanging out together."

I shrug and smile, as if painting with an elephant is just an ordinary everyday thing in my life.

"I was hanging out at my mom's trapeze school," Henry Jack says. "Your mom is working there today."

"I know." I rinse the brushes as Queenie Grace lumbers away.

"She was bragging about a painting that you did of your grandpa," Henry Jack reports. "I must have heard about it a hundred times today."

Trullia was bragging . . . about me?

"My mom was bragging about you, too," Henry Jack continues. "Telling everybody about the painting you did of me, showing it to them. She took a picture of it with her phone camera after she hung it on the wall at our place. It made her cry when she first saw it."

"I'm not sure if that's good or bad," I say. "My art making people cry."

"It's good," Henry Jack says. "Because your paintings are touching their hearts. It's your gift, Lily."

I'm not very good at accepting compliments, and so I just keep swishing paintbrushes in the cup, watching the water change colors.

"How much for this painting?" Henry Jack asks. "I'd like to buy it. First original by Lily Pruitt and the Amazing Queenie Grace."

"Free for you," I reply. "It's my gift."

Henry Jack is hanging the painting on his bedroom wall when his mother gets home from work.

"Look at the painting that Lily did with Queenie Grace," he says.

"Oh, how sweet," says Faith. "It's beautiful!"

"She gave it to me," Henry Jack reports. "I offered to buy it. . . ."

"It's a gift," I say. "Merry Christmas, two days late."

"Oh, Lily," says Faith. "I can't thank you enough. Not only

for this painting, but for the one you did yesterday of Henry Jack. Well, let's just say I've been blinking back tears ever since I saw it."

I smile. Faith is studying Henry Jack's face.

"That sunburn doesn't look good," she says, peering at his skin.

He sighs.

"I don't want you going outside in the sunshine for a few days," Faith says to Henry Jack.

"Can I go out at night?" he asks. "Like tonight?"

"Yes, but no later than ten o'clock," Faith says. "Remember, the funeral is tomorrow."

My stomach lurches. I don't have to try to remember; I have to try to forget.

Henry Jack and Queenie Grace and I hang together in the yard, by the tree. Henry Jack and I stretch flat on our backs, staring up at the nighttime sky. Queenie Grace towers over us, as if standing guard. She's blocking the moon, but I can still see stars.

"So I'm really nervous for tomorrow," I say. "For the, you know, the . . . funeral."

"Yeah, well, funerals are never exactly fun," says Henry Jack. I look at him. He's staring straight up.

"Even though I know funerals have a bright side, I still couldn't help but hate my brother's funeral," Henry Jack says.

"That's when it all became so totally final. And now I just talk to him in the stars, in the sky, at night."

We're both quiet for a few minutes.

"That's so sad," I say, finally breaking the silence. "Do you really think he's up there?"

"Where else would he be?" asks Henry Jack.

We fall silent again, like paying our respects to Henry Jack's dead twin. Even Queenie Grace is breathing quieter, standing still except for her trunk, which sways back and forth, back and forth.

"I'm going to try to believe that's true," I say. "I'm going to have faith that my grandpa is okay, that he is really up there. Still with us, except in a different way."

"Love doesn't die," says Henry Jack.

"Okay," I say. "This conversation is getting a little too deep for me."

We both laugh: another *we're in this together* moment. Nothing like talking about dead people to bond a friendship.

"You know what's kind of cool?" I say. "I'm less afraid already."

"Afraid of . . . ?"

"Everything. Well, the elephant mostly."

"I told you, Lily Rose," says Henry Jack. "There is nothing to be afraid of, especially when it comes to Queenie Grace."

"Well, if you knew what I went through when I was six, when she almost killed me . . ."

"*Pfffft*. Queenie Grace would never hurt a kid. She'd never hurt *anybody*!"

"That's what you think. We all have our opinions. And my opinion is that elephants are dangerous."

"What about humans? They're dangerous, too."

"Yes," I agree. "They can be."

Just then, there's a high yelp from somewhere nearby. Henry Jack and I both sit up, quickly.

"Was that a kid?" I ask.

"I don't know," Henry Jack replies.

Queenie Grace looks around. She heard it, too: the squeal from something little. Something that's hurt.

Sitting quietly in the dark, eyes like telescopes, Henry Jack and I both turn our heads in the direction of the sound. The yelps are coming from Fire-Eating Charlie's house.

"Holy showman," whispers Henry Jack. "He's hitting his dogs."

I see it, too. The sheer curtains are drawn, but the light is on, and we can see silhouettes. Fire-Eating Charlie is holding each one up, dog by dog, smacking them.

"Bad!" he shouts. "You don't chew on carpet!"

I clench my teeth, watching mean, evil Charlie. His wife Mary is nowhere to be seen, and neither is mean Mike. Finally, Charlie stops smacking the dogs, and next thing you know, the front door opens. He walks out, slow, onto his porch: *clunk, clunk, clunk.*

"He's wearing spurs on his boots," Henry Jack whispers. "He does that sometimes. My mom says he rode Queenie Grace wearing spurs, and kicked her in the sides. He'd dig in with those sharp spurs, trying to make her move faster. Called himself the Elephant Cowboy. He did it like three times, until your Grandpa Bill found out and put a stop to it."

"I despise him," I whisper. "I despise that man Charlie with every cell in my body."

Queenie Grace is shaking a little bit.

"Me too," Henry Jack responds. "We all do."

Queenie Grace
Remembers the Spurs

I remember the spurs. I remember the sharp metal digging into my skin, Fire-Eating Charlie kicking. It hurt.

Bill punched Charlie in the face when he caught him riding me with the spurs. Bill the Giant was a gentle man, but not when it came to somebody hurting me.

I can still see Bill's fist meeting Charlie's cheek. *Pow!* It made a nice, satisfying sound.

I never felt the spurs again. But tonight, Charlie wears them again. The sound makes me shiver. It makes me shake.

Funeral Day

This funeral home smells like flowers, the dust from old tissues, and strong perfume. There are paintings of angels in golden frames, and bouquets of flowers all over the place, plus my painting of Grandpa Bill, propped up on a metal stand. The room is packed, and I actually know some people: Grandma. Trullia. Mike. Henry Jack. His mom, Faith. George. Mary, the Bearded Lady. And of course, mean Fire-Eating Charlie. He's wearing the spurs again, and it sounds like death in a Western movie when he walks on the wooden floor of the funeral home.

Grandma, Trullia, and I are lined up beside the casket, greeting people like this is a party. A line of three, all related by blood. I'm trying not to look at Grandpa Bill's abandoned body.

The windows are open and you can hear birds chirping, like this is any old ordinary morning. The birds don't know any better, and neither do the people driving by in their cars. The sky is blue and the sun shines. The world just goes on like normal, while the little universe of its own inside the funeral home is all about time standing still.

This part of the service is the viewing. It's where people look at the body.

"It helps the family to accept that the person really is gone, and to find closure," Grandma Violet explained to me last night. "It helps the loved ones to go on."

Not me. I don't feel like accepting or finding "closure" or going on anywhere. Not without Grandpa Bill.

So I just stand there beside the casket and greet people, a wet and crumpled tissue clutched in my hand. Everyone keeps raving about how tall I am, how much I look like Grandma, how much they loved Grandpa Bill, how I was the apple of his eye.

Sometimes, over some stranger's shoulder, I catch a glimpse of Henry Jack, sitting in one of the chairs. Every time I meet his eye, he tries to smile and he gives a little nod, like saying, *It's all right. Go on. You're doing fine. Breathe. You'll be okay.*

Seeing Henry Jack's face is keeping me sane.

It's time for the service, and pictures of Grandpa Bill are projected onto a screen. Grandma sits in a folding chair on one side of me. Henry Jack's on the other. Trullia hides somewhere in the very back. I can hear her hacking, and the sound of Mike clearing his throat.

We're in the very front, so now I can't help seeing Grandpa Bill, all laid out in that casket. He looks like a creepy wax version of my grandfather, and I keep imagining what would happen if he just sat up and started talking. That would totally freak me out.

"I keep thinking I see his heart beating," I whisper to Henry Jack. "Like something is moving on the side of his neck."

"A trick of the eyes," Henry Jack whispers back. "It's just what you wish was happening."

I'm wearing the jeweled pink flip-flops and the nice flowered sundress from Trullia, and Henry Jack is sporting a dark blue suit. His tie is splashed with old cartoons from the 1960s.

My grandma cries really hard but quietly, shaking with trying to keep it inside. Her hair is in a braid, and she's wearing a long tie-dyed hippie skirt and a black T-shirt. She grabs my hand every now and then, which makes me have to bite my cheek. *I will not cry, I will not cry, I will not cry. I will keep it inside.*

A funeral director—a tall bald man in a crisp black suit—conducts the service. He includes Bible verses along with funny little stories about my grandpa, like how one time he tried to run a marathon but had to stop. There's the song "Amazing Grace," and I can hear people blowing their noses and snorting. I guess other people try not to cry, too.

The song comes to an end and the beehive-hairdo lady named Kathryn who is playing the piano gets up and clicks in little red pointy heels back to her seat. There's an awkward silence, with just the nose honking and the snorting.

A horrible noise trumpets suddenly from outside. It sounds like a combination of a monster blowing his nose and the sky falling and an airplane crashing. Some people put their hands to their ears and others look at one another, all puzzled and scared. One man stands, as if he's going to save the world.

And then I see the source of all that racket: Queenie Grace, standing near a window behind my grandfather's body. She's looking straight in at the casket, and she's wailing at the top of her lungs.

I look at my grandmother. She seems to be in shock. Henry Jack leans forward to look at Grandma, too, then he looks at me. I mouth the word "wow."

Grandma pulls herself up from her seat with a heavy sigh, swishing in her long skirt to the exit door.

People turn around to watch. A somber silence hangs heavy in the room. Trullia gets up from the back row, mouth turned down, and she follows Grandma outside. Mike hustles out, too.

At least all this excitement has made some people stop crying.

Queenie Grace Does Not Like Dead

I see Bill. I see his body, my *mahout*, my trainer, my keeper. I see Bill the Giant, my best friend, and he is dead. He does not smell like Bill!

I remember dead, from that other country. There was a place there, a spot where elephants went to die. We paid our respect to the bones there, in that place. Sometimes we carried those bones, showing reverence.

Oh, I want to break that window and lift Bill from that box. I want to bring him back to life, to make him smile, to hear his voice.

But I cannot make this happen. Maybe someone else can bring Bill back to life. Maybe I can make them listen. Maybe they will help.

I scream as loudly as I can. I lift my trunk to the sky,

and I cry. I swing my trunk like something that can hit; like something that can hurt. I am so, so angry.

People stare at me. I would like to break that window, but I remember the trouble with the window and the pack of peanuts. I will not cause that trouble again.

Violet bursts outside. Grief erupts from her eyes. And then Trullia and Mike storm into view.

"Go home!" Mike shouts. He points in the direction of the trailer.

I lower my head, shake it.

And then Mike smacks me. I have never before been hit. I've been burned, and I've been spurred. But I've never been hit, not here.

I do not like this. I try not to cry, but I feel it: a tear.

Violet draws herself up stiff and straight. She crosses her arms and sets her face like a stone.

"How dare you hit her?" she says to Mike. "She's only expressing her feelings! You will not touch her again, you hear me?"

Mike's eyes grow wide.

"She's disrupting your husband's funeral," he hisses. "She doesn't belong here."

"She belongs here as much as any one of us who loved Bill," Violet shouts. "If there's anybody who doesn't belong, it's *you!*"

"Mom," says Trullia. "Calm down. People can hear."

Violet rolls her eyes.

I raise my trunk into the sky, and I let out a loud cry. I bellow. I shout to the sky about everything that makes me feel so alone.

I shout to the sky, but there is no answer.

The Sound of an Elephant
with a Broken Heart

I see it through the window: Mike hits Queenie Grace. I flinch when Mike's hand meets elephant skin. Grandma keeps her arms crossed as if trying to hold her heart inside.

I sit straight up in shock and worry, and so does Henry Jack.

Queenie Grace bellows. Grandma stands up straight and yells at Mike; Trullia yells at Grandma.

The people in the funeral home get all awkward and uncomfortable, shuffling and shifting in their seats. The funeral home man closes the lid of the casket.

A tear slips from my eye, and Henry Jack pats my back. That makes it worse, and more runaway tears escape.

I will never again see that face.

I bite my cheek. *I will not cry, not again; I won't. Nope. I'll keep it inside. Keep it inside where it belongs.*

We shamble outside, in a line. Some people cry; others hug.

"I'm sorry," people say to Grandma and me. I feel as if so many people care: about me, about Grandma Violet, about Grandpa Bill. If sorry could bring my grandpa back to life, he'd be standing here smiling.

We go through the parking lot to where men in suits have placed little white flags of surrender on the cars that are going to the cemetery. Trullia's car has a flag, and we all pile in.

Trullia drives. Her eyes are red and hard in the rearview mirror. Nobody talks and there's just the sound of wheels on road. The turn signal, the squeak of the brakes.

Queenie Grace follows behind the line of slow-moving cars. She trudges along as if she's a vehicle, too, part of this sad car parade. She follows us all the way to the Restful Souls Cemetery, and then she waits outside the curved iron gates.

We park outside of the graveyard. Everybody gets out of their cars, including us. It starts to rain, tiny droplets, but the sun still shines. A few people pop open umbrellas.

The casket is brought out of the hearse. Men with respectful expressions carry the coffin and place it carefully under a green tent.

There's talking, prayers, flowers, bowed heads, tissues. Grandma clutches her hands into fists.

And then it's all over. He's in the ground, forever and ever. Grandpa Bill is gone.

We are all leaving the cemetery, just as Queenie Grace is going in. She plods determinedly through the gates and straight over to the open hole of earth that holds her best friend in a blue box. She lowers herself slowly to the ground, huge body trembling.

Queenie Grace just lies on the cool, damp ground, sprawled over that open rectangle shape in the earth.

Queenie Grace Wants Bill

Billlllll. I refuse to move. Oh, how I need my *mahout.*

Amazing Grace

Nobody can make the elephant move from the grave. Not even Henry Jack. They are trying all kinds of things, but nothing works. Queenie Grace just lies there, over the grave.

"Jeez," says Henry Jack. "She always listens to me. She's definitely not herself."

"That's what I've been saying," Grandma says. "Grief changes you."

"What are we going to do?" Trullia asks. "How will we get her out of here?"

And then I remember: Grandpa Bill's song, the one that always made Queenie Grace follow.

I whistle "Amazing Grace," just like I remember Grandpa doing it, that last time in West Virginia.

Queenie Grace looks at me. And then, she slowly, slowly,

slowly heaves herself up to standing.

I keep whistling. I start to walk, and she follows me. She follows me all the way out of the cemetery, onto the road. I just keep walking, never looking back, hearing the weight of Queenie Grace behind me.

When I get to the car, I do Grandpa's tongue-click sound for *stop*, and she listens. Queenie Grace listens to me and she stops, right behind the little green car.

"Lily," whispers Grandma Violet. "You are just like your grandpa. Why, I think she listens to you almost as well as she listened to Bill. You have the magic touch."

We all get in the car. Trullia drives again, her eyes checking the rearview mirror for the elephant. She's still following the car.

Queenie Grace follows the car all the way home.

Queenie Grace Knows Bill's Song

I know Bill's song. That is something I will never forget. And the girl Lily whistles it just right. Just like Bill.

How to Save an Elephant

Slumped on the porch with Henry Jack, I feel drained, as if the funeral sucked all the life out of me. My eyes hurt from crying, I'm tired, and my heart pings lonely with the missing of my grandpa.

We slurp red Popsicles, and Henry Jack's lips are stained. Luckily, the sky is cloudy and we don't have to worry as much about sunburn for Henry Jack. Queenie Grace huddles in the yard, back on the chain because she already tried to run back to the grave. Queenie Grace bawls and bellows. The sound booms like thunder.

"I never heard such a terrible noise," comments Henry Jack.

I nod. "It's horrible," I say. "Goes right through me."

Queenie Grace eyes us and stops making the sounds.

She just stares, her eyes meeting mine, and something about those eyes makes me care a lot about this elephant. It's like there's an invisible thread between us, pulling, connecting, joining.

"I can't believe my grandma chained her again," I comment.

"I know," Henry Jack agrees. "But she really did have to do something to keep her here. I think she'd just keep running back to Bill. To the cemetery."

"She's so sad," I say.

"I know. It's like you can feel her soul, right? Nothing like the soul of an elephant: it's big and fluffy and floaty, kind of like those clouds."

I look up at the sky. Gray storm clouds have gathered, and they're shifting and changing shapes before our eyes.

Trullia appears at the screen door, a bag of chips in her hand.

"You two need a snack?" she asks.

"No, thanks," I say.

"Not hungry," Henry Jack says.

"I know, me neither," Trullia says. "Who feels like eating on a day like this, right?"

She goes back inside.

"I feel bad for her," Henry Jack says. "She lost her dad. I know how that feels."

"Yeah. I know how it feels, too. The losing feeling."

"By the way," says Henry Jack, "you did a good job at the funeral."

"A 'good job'? How can you do a good job at a funeral?"

"Well, like, you were so polite to everybody and you held it together and stayed strong for your grandma."

"My dad taught me to be polite," I reply. "And I taught myself how to hold it together. As far as being strong, not so much. I could bawl from now till my flight home, if I let myself."

I stare at Queenie Grace, then close my eyes for a few seconds. The shape of the elephant remains on the back of my eyelids.

"Did you ever notice how you can stare at something," I say to Henry Jack, "then close your eyes and have it stay there, on your eyelids?"

"Of course," Henry Jack says. "Hasn't everybody?"

"I don't know. But now I have an elephant in my eyes."

"Well, that's better than an elephant in the room. You know, like how they say, 'There's an elephant in the room' when nobody talks about the obvious bad thing?"

I nod.

Trullia and Grandma have moved into the kitchen, and their voices strain out through the screen window.

"I'm afraid that we might have to . . . send her away," says my grandmother. "It kills me to say that, because Bill would never have stood for it. But I don't know how we're going to feed an elephant, now that we don't have the act anymore. The account's very low, and the electric bill is due. Plus the lot rent."

"But where would she go?" asks Trullia.

Henry Jack looks at me.

"They're thinking of putting Queenie Grace in an old folks' home," he says, low. "An old folks' home for elephants."

"Well, there's that nice new elephant sanctuary up near Tampa," Grandma says. "I've heard they take great care of them there. And they're free to roam, make friends, and enjoy their later years."

"See?" Henry Jack mutters. "Told you. That's what happened to this other elephant I remember from when I was little, named Thunder."

"But why not make some money?" asks Trullia. "Sell her to another circus or something?"

"No," Grandma says. "She had her career, and it was with Bill. And anyway, didn't you know that even Ringling Brothers stopped their elephant acts? They realized that not all elephants enjoy the work of being in a circus. Queenie Grace loved her job, but she loved it because it was with Bill. It wouldn't be fair to team her up with somebody new at this age. Plus, I couldn't trust just anybody. I want to be sure that she's loved and that somebody takes good care of her."

"Well, how do we know the elephant sanctuary will take her?" Trullia asks.

"I called them yesterday," says Grandma. "That was one call I didn't want to make, but sometimes a person just has no choice."

There's the sound of the chip bag being ripped open, crunching.

"We just can't afford Queenie Grace anymore," Grandma says.

"Well, yeah, you're right, I guess. Plus, she has been acting out a bit, we have to admit," Trullia adds.

"I know that Queenie Grace is grieving," says Grandma, her voice breaking like dropped china. "So am I. I understand that. And now I'm not only grieving for Bill, but for her, too. She's been with us for a long time. I love that elephant like I love a child."

"I think that maybe you love her more than you love me," Trullia says.

Nobody speaks. Silence falls heavy as storm clouds gather in a threatening gang over Gibtown, over Grandma's trailer, over me and Henry Jack and Queenie Grace.

Nighttime again, and Henry Jack and I are lying flat on our backs, staring at the quiet sky in our usual spot. Queenie Grace is sprawled nearby, an aura of sadness hanging over her large body.

"I think she knows," Henry Jack says. "She knows what's going on."

A screen door squeaks, and Mike steps out of Charlie's place. He doesn't know we're here. He joins Charlie in the yard, and they both light cigars.

"So," Mike says, "here's the plan. The old lady says she's sending the elephant to a sanctuary, over in Tampa, on account of how she can't afford it anymore."

"How do you know?" Charlie asks.

"Trullia told me."

"When's it happening?" Charlie asks.

"Probably by Saturday," says Mike. "But I have a plan."

"Let's hear it."

"We load up the elephant while the old lady and Trullia are sleeping," says Mike, "and then we split the money three ways. You, me, our buddy Gus. Takes three to swipe an elephant."

Henry Jack looks at me and I look at him, as we absorb the words leaking through the night.

"They're . . . going to steal Queenie Grace," I whisper.

"Not if I can help it," Henry Jack mutters.

He and I lock eyes, and I know we're thinking the same thing.

"We've got to get her out of here," I state. "We've got to save Queenie Grace."

We're quiet until Mike and Charlie go back inside.

"We need to tell my grandma," I whisper.

"No," Henry Jack whispers back. "Then she'll just send Queenie Grace away even quicker, to keep her away from those two."

"So," I whisper, "what are we going to do?"

"Run away," he whispers. "We'll take Queenie Grace."

"But how can you run away with an *elephant*?"

"Beats me," says Henry Jack. "But we'll figure it out."

"I don't know," I say. "Doesn't sound like much of a plan."

"Sometimes it's best not to plan," responds Henry Jack. "Plus, we don't have much time. Queenie Grace's life is at stake."

"I know. But jeez. I don't know about running away. My dad would freak out. Plus my grandma. And Trullia . . . she'll be so mad."

"I just can't get used to you calling her Trullia," says Henry Jack.

"That's her name."

"But . . . she's your mom. You need to call her Mom."

"If she ever earns it," I say, "I'll do that."

"Huh," says Henry Jack. "Never heard of that."

I shrug.

"So what does she have to do? To earn it?"

I take a deep breath. Queenie Grace watches us, eavesdropping.

"Well," I say, "to begin with, maybe she can explain why she went and left us."

Henry Jack snorts.

"Some things in life," he says, flipping back his hair, "just can't be explained."

The next morning, Friday, we're making a list, or at least, Henry Jack is. *How to Save an Elephant. Things to Take* is the title.

1. water bottles
2. food (stuff for us and Queenie Grace, too)
3. sunburn stuff
4. soap/washcloths
5. *Manual for Mahouts*
6. blankets
7. change of clothes
8. cell phones
9. chargers
10. toothbrushes/toothpaste

We're at Henry Jack's house, and he's filling four backpacks with things from the list.

"I think we need more than backpacks," I say. "We need like rolling suitcases or something."

"Oh, like that won't be obvious," says Henry Jack. "One elephant and two kids with rolling luggage."

"Well, how are we going to carry all this stuff?"

"Queenie Grace will help," Henry Jack says. "We'll use

this howdah thing that I know is stored in your grandma's pink shed."

"What's a howdah?"

"It's one of those saddle-like thingies that people use to ride an elephant," Henry Jack explains. "But we can use it to carry some stuff."

"And how will we get it on Queenie Grace's back?"

"Duh," says Henry Jack. "We'll use a ladder."

"This all sounds like a stupid plan to me."

"No," Henry Jack said. "It's the opposite of stupid. It's smart. We'll save Queenie Grace."

"Henry Jack," I say, "I agree we have to save her. But this running-away thing might not be a good idea. It might be impossible."

"Nothing," says Henry Jack, cramming a rolled-up blanket into a third backpack, "is impossible."

Queenie Grace Hates to Feel Hate

I hate these chains. I have never felt hate this strong before. Hate is a bad feeling.

Nighttime has fallen, and Violet and Trullia are sleeping. I smell their sleep, and I hear their breath. I always liked the sound of Bill's sleep. Now that he no longer breathes, I miss the air from his nose, from his mouth. I just miss Bill.

I can now smell the girl Lily and Henry Jack, the Alligator Boy. They do not sleep, and their breath huffs heavy. Henry Jack and Lily come closer, and each one holds bags on their back. Each one wears a cap the color of night, and clothes like nighttime sky. They are trying not to be seen, and they are trying to be quiet. Their feet are not bare, and I hear their shoe bottoms scoot across the dew-coated grass.

The Alligator Boy carries something—a sharp hacksaw.

He kneels down as if to pray, and then he begins to saw away at my chains.

I raise my trunk. *I must be quiet! I must be still! I must wait for Henry Jack to break the chains!*

I no longer feel hate.

Running Away

Henry Jack leads the way. I try to be silent, and I guess Queenie Grace is being as quiet as possible for such a gigantic creature. She moves fast, swinging her trunk back and forth, a little grin on her lips. If you could call them lips, that is. Her breathing snuffles loud in the night; her weight moves the earth. It looks like she swivels her hips, as if she's doing an elephant tango. We actually managed to get the howdah on her back, with the help of one of Grandpa's old stepladders.

"She looks sassy," I say. "Happy."

"She is happy," Henry Jack responds. "Aren't you?"

"Not exactly. There's got to be a better way to save Queenie Grace."

"Well, when you come up with it," says Henry Jack, "you

just let me know."

We pass trailers all lit up with Christmas lights, and others dark and quiet. I catch a glimpse of a lady wearing a long white nightgown in a lit-up window, and another in a robe. It smells like summertime. We pass by the abandoned Ferris wheel, silhouetted against the nighttime sky, and there's the spooky sound of old-fashioned carousel music coming from out of nowhere.

"That old carousel actually works?" I whisper to Henry Jack.

"Sometimes," says Henry Jack, "it just starts up all by itself."

I shiver.

"That's creepy," I say. "Maybe it's haunted."

"Well, ghosts aren't what we need to be afraid of," says Henry Jack. "It's some of the living people who are the scariest. Like Charlie and Mike."

"Okay," I say, "you're freaking me out. Let's change the subject now."

"Okay. We'll chat about running away."

"Or not."

We walk and walk, Queenie Grace lumbering between us, out of Gibtown, until there's hard highway beneath our feet.

"Jeez," I say. "That was easy."

"Nothing's easy," says Henry Jack. "It's not like it's over

yet. Not over till the fat lady sings, Mom always says."

Queenie Grace makes a little sound, as if she's laughing.

"She has a great sense of humor," I say.

"That's what my mom always says, too," replies Henry Jack. "She says Queenie Grace is the most human elephant she ever met."

"It's true," I say. "She's more human than some people I know."

Henry Jack snickers.

"True," he says.

"So, where are we going, anyway?" I ask.

"You're too full of questions," Henry Jack says. "Sometimes it's better to just follow the stars without talking so much, like the Wise Men. Especially when you're with somebody who knows what he's doing and knows where he's going."

"You're awfully sure of yourself," I say.

"Hey," says Henry Jack, "when you're born with alligator skin, you learn how to be strong."

We trudge on and on, off the highway and onto a dark fairy-tale trail through woods. Briars scratch my arms; limbs snap at my face. I'm tired, I'm hungry, I'm thirsty, I'm scared, I'm hot.

I'm wheezing; breathing sure isn't easy. *I might die.*

Queenie Grace looks at me, as if she's reading my mind.

I feel the nuzzle of her trunk against my leg. She reminds me of Donna on the airplane: just giving me a little touch to let me know that everything will be okay. Queenie Grace is starting to feel almost like a lady to me, an old, quiet, and kind lady, maybe a spiritual adviser like Miss Donna.

Maybe Queenie Grace is a human communicator: she figures out the souls of people.

Queenie Grace Is Old, But She Loves to Feel Alive

I am romping, happy to be free. I love being here, in the woods, by the creek, under the moon and stars! I love the crunching beneath my feet, the snap of twigs. I love the musky smell of the forest.

Being free, being with my friends, makes me feel alive. I finally feel fully alive, for the first time since Bill died.

We are running away, they say. I do not know exactly what this means, but for now, it feels good.

And that is why I try to ignore the smell of the smoke, of the fire, of the danger smoldering nearby.

The Men with Fire

"So what's the plan?" I ask. "I'm really feeling like this isn't such a good idea."

"You worry too much, Lily Rose," says Henry Jack. "Look at the bright side: so far everything has gone just fine."

"So far," I reply, "we've only been gone like an hour."

"I don't need this kind of negativity," Henry Jack says, and then he snickers. "You need to relax."

"It's not very relaxing to run away with an elephant in the middle of the night!" I say. "What exactly are we going to do, anyway?"

"I'm thinking of a place where we can maybe hide her here, in the woods, at least until we tell your grandma what we heard Mike and Charlie say. And then we talk her into giving it another try with Queenie Grace, after calling the cops on Mike and Charlie."

"That's not going to work. And anyway, how long can you hide an elephant?"

Nervousness gnaws away at me. Henry Jack says nothing; he just walks with his head bent forward and down.

"Seriously," I say, "we can't exactly *hide* her. She's enormous! Plus, like, she has to be fed a lot, and watered, and . . ."

Henry Jack stops walking. He looks at me.

"You may be right," he says. "Maybe we do need a better plan."

"So can we go back and talk about this some more? Maybe tell my grandma what's going on?"

He sighs.

"All right," he says. "You talked me into it."

But then he puts his nose up in the air like a bloodhound.

"I smell cigar smoke," Henry Jack hisses. "I have a nose for Charlie the Fire-Eater. He's somewhere close, I'd bet you a million dollars."

"I don't smell it," I whisper. There's a breeze and leaves rustle on the trees. It's spooky here, in the woods, at night. We're at least a mile from Grandma's place, and we've been walking for ages. We forgot to bring a flashlight.

"I smell it," Henry Jack says. "I can smell Charlie a mile away."

He pats Queenie Grace's back.

"Still," he says gently to the elephant. "Be still, Queenie Grace."

She obeys, standing motionless as an elephant can stand, moving nothing but her ears. I feel the slight breeze from the flapping of those big ears.

Henry Jack tips back his head, listening, sniffing.

"Okay," he whispers. "My radar nose has it figured out. I smell campfire smoke, plus Charlie's cigar. We need to get the heck out of here. Follow me."

My heart races. I'm dizzy.

"Walk as lightly as you can," Henry Jack instructs. "That means you, too, Queenie Grace."

Henry Jack, Queenie Grace, and I try to walk lightly in the direction of my grandma's place, clenching our teeth as twigs snap and crack beneath our feet.

"Shh," he says. "Dang, we're going in the wrong direction. My nose failed me, for once."

"What do you mean?" I whisper. My heart hammers in my ears. We three come to a stop. Branches brush against my face.

"See?"

Through the trees and the leaves, there's the flicker of fire. Orange: a campfire, flaming high.

"It's him," Henry Jack whispers. "He's eating fire, see?"

I do see. Charlie wears his cowboy hat. He tips his head

back, swallows the fire. Mike's here, too, and another man we don't know.

"Must be Gus," Henry Jack whispers. "The Gus he mentioned."

"So how much money will we make?" asks the stranger.

"A lot," Charlie replies. "Plenty. More money that I've seen in a heck of a long time."

"More money than *we've* seen," Mike says. "Split three ways, remember?"

Henry Jack nudges me. He points and mouths the word "Run."

We do. Henry Jack and Queenie Grace and me. We run as fast as we can, as far as we can, thundering through the forest, and then we stop to catch our breath at the edge of the woods. Queenie Grace is trembling.

"Don't worry," says Henry Jack to the elephant. "We'll take care of you, girl. We'll protect you. Saving you is our number one priority."

Something buzzes around my face: a mosquito or a bee. I didn't think they came out at night. I slap it away, and next thing you know, Queenie Grace turns and stampedes right back into the woods, crashing through branches.

"Queenie Grace!" Henry Jack yells. "Stop!"

She keeps going.

"We've got to get her!" Henry Jack says. "Come on!"

Queenie Grace tramples loudly through the woods, right in the direction of the three men and the campfire. We chase after her.

"Stop," hisses Henry Jack. "Stop, Queenie Grace."

But the elephant doesn't listen. We run fast as we can after her, but she just keeps on going and next thing you know, we're at the fire. The flames light Queenie Grace's face.

"Hey!" yells Mike. "There it is! What the heck . . ."

The man Gus jumps up. He lunges for Queenie Grace. So do Mike, and Charlie, the three of them all going at once for Queenie Grace. Three grown men against one old elephant.

I draw in a breath, terrified. I try to grab Henry Jack.

But he's moving too fast. Henry Jack leaps forward, jumping on Mike's back.

"Get off me!" Mike yells. The man Gus raises his fist and I see three letters tattooed into his knuckles: G U S.

"Don't hit the kid!" Charlie shouts. "What do you want, to get arrested?"

I'm screaming and screaming, and finally realize that I do have a phone for emergencies. And this is an emergency. But then I remember: the phone is only for text messages. You can't exactly text 911.

Queenie Grace knocks Gus to the ground with her trunk. Henry Jack scrambles up; so does Mike.

"Get him!" Mike yells. Charlie wraps an arm around Henry Jack's waist, holding him tight.

Queenie Grace whacks Charlie with her trunk, and then she puts one foot on the man Gus, pinning him to the ground, protecting Henry Jack and protecting herself and protecting me. You can tell that she's not placing much weight on Gus. She's just keeping him down.

She keeps him there, on the ground, in the woods.

Queenie Grace Is Afraid

I am afraid! This man Gus smells like danger.

I lift my trunk and I whack Charlie, hard on the back. I hit him so hard and fast, and something falls from his hand.

The man Gus raises his fist at me.

That's when Henry Jack leaps forward like a wildcat. He leaps on Mike's back and makes him fall to the ground.

"Get off me!" Mike yells.

I lift one foot, raise my hoof, and I hold the man Gus tight to the ground. I push just hard enough to keep him down, but not to hurt him. I pin that bad man to the ground and I don't budge.

Queenie Grace Saves Me

Charlie is still holding Henry Jack, despite the whack from Queenie Grace.

"Run, Lily!" Henry Jack yells. "Get out of here! Go get help!"

I don't want to run. I don't want to leave Queenie Grace and Henry Jack with these three men.

"Lily, run!" Henry Jack says, teeth clenched. Charlie's arms are circling his waist. Henry Jack kicks, and spits.

So I do. I run. I have never been so scared in my entire life. It's like fear struck my body like lightning. I'm wheezing so bad. I can hardly breathe. I can hardly run anymore.

And then I trip. My foot kicks a big rock and I fall forward, scraping my face on rocks and leaves and branches from trees. I try to stand. I must have twisted my ankle, and I sit back down.

I hear the ground pounding behind me, and I hear the sounds of sticks breaking. The men are coming; they are running. They will get me.

I try to stand again. I can't. I just can't. I think my right ankle is broken.

"Help," I whisper to nobody in particular. "Please help."

Queenie Grace crashes through the woods and comes to my side, studying the situation for a quick minute, and then she reaches down with her trunk. She gently pushes her trunk under my back, and then lifts, slowly, slowly, until I am folded snug.

"What in the world . . . ?" I say. This feels like a bad dream. I am wrapped in an elephant's trunk, in the woods, with a broken ankle and three bad men who are probably killing my friend. And then they will get me, and it'll all be over. That's how my story will end, here in Florida, in the woods, far away from my dad and my home. There is no bright side to this, no happy ending.

I close my eyes. Queenie Grace is making a low purring sound in her throat. I feel as if maybe she's saying, *Relax. I've got this.*

There's nothing to hold on to when you're wrapped in an elephant's trunk. It's like a crazy amusement park ride where you just buckle in and trust that you'll be okay in the end.

Queenie Grace runs. I'm jostled, a lot. I don't think she will let me fall.

"Be careful," I say. She's holding me like a baby, like a giant baby who's cradled in a parent's big, soft, safe arms.

I bounce and bump, jostled and bobbled, carried by only the trunk of an elephant who's running for all she's worth.

"Thank you, Queenie Grace," I say. "Thank you. I love you."

Queenie Grace Loves Lily, Too

I left Henry Jack when I heard Lily's cries. I will save this girl if it's the last thing I do. Inside my head, I hear my best friend Bill's voice. He says, *Run, Queenie Grace! Save Lily!*

And so I do. I pick Lily up with my trunk and I run. I always did listen to Bill.

I wish I could have picked up Henry Jack, too. Perhaps I will get Lily back safely, and return for Henry Jack.

"Be careful!" Lily says. She is frightened. But she need not worry: this is a trick I learned in the circus. I know how to carry a person, safe and snug, wrapped up with my trunk. I have never dropped anybody yet. And I certainly won't drop Lily.

"Thank you, Queenie Grace," Lily says. "Thank you. I love you."

Those are words Bill always said. I can still hear him inside my head. I see his face inside my mind. He smiles. Oh, how I once loved my best friend Bill.

And now, I love the girl Lily, too.

A Long Story

Queenie Grace runs all the way home, back to Grandma's. She deposits me ever so slowly and carefully onto the ground.

I try to stand. Finally, I heave myself up, and I limp to the door, hopping mostly on my left leg.

I burst through the door. To my surprise, Grandma and Trullia are awake, watching TV. They both gawk at me, jaws falling.

"Why are you guys up so late?" I ask.

"We were both having trouble sleeping," Trullia says.

"Lily!" says Grandma. "Why is your face all scratched up? Why, honey, you're all bloody!"

"What the heck . . . ?" says Trullia.

"Call 911!" I gasp. "Tell them to go into the woods, past a

pond, I think. It's sort of in the middle where there's a camp-fire circle. Mike and Charlie and this other guy have Henry Jack. Call . . . quick."

"What do you mean, they have . . . ," Grandma says. She looks so confused, frozen as if she's in shock.

"Please, just call! I'll explain later!"

Trullia picks up her phone. She calls. Her voice is pretty calm. I think maybe she thinks I'm exaggerating.

Grandma gets off the sofa and comes to hug me.

"Oh, honey, are you okay?" she asks.

I nod.

"Queenie Grace carried me."

"Oh, she used to do that with your grandpa. I think it was her favorite trick."

Trullia is off the phone.

"I'm surprised you didn't just ride on her back," she says.

"Well, there were all the backpacks. . . ."

"What was Queenie Grace doing with backpacks?"

"Long story. I'll tell you later."

"And you said that Charlie and Mike are in the woods, and they have Henry Jack?"

I nod.

"I told you," Grandma barks. "I told you that man was no good!"

"So why were you and Henry Jack and Queenie Grace in

the woods in the first place?" Trullia demands.

"It's . . . a long story. Can we please go meet the police in the woods?"

"I can hear you breathing," says Grandma. "Wheezing. I think you need to go to the hospital. What's wrong with your leg?"

"I fell. I think I broke my ankle."

"Oh, jeez," says Trullia. "One thing after another."

They hustle me outside, Grandma's arm reaching up to circle my waist. I can hear sirens. The police are on their way.

Mary the Bearded Lady comes out of her trailer.

"What's going on?" she calls across the yard.

"Explain later!" Grandma shouts. "It's a long story."

Queenie Grace Watches Them Go

Violet and Trullia and Lily pile into the car. There was talk of the hospital, of returning to the woods.

I pray that Henry Jack is okay. I wish I could have saved him, too.

I heard the words of the three bad men. I know their plans to steal me, to take me away, to make big money from the Amazing Queenie Grace.

If not for my friends, my two best friends, I might have been dead. I might have been gone, sold to a circus that would not treat me well.

Thank you, I say to my friends inside my head.

I watch them go. I watch the car until the red lights disappear into the night.

An Emergency as Big
as an Elephant

They've sent plenty of vehicles. Parked at the edge of the trees are three police cruisers, an ambulance, a fire truck. Lights flash; sirens blare. Men and women storm into the forest, carrying medical equipment.

"Let's go with them," I say to Grandma.

"Lily," she says, "you have an injured ankle."

"I don't care. I need to see that Henry Jack is all right."

And so we head into the thick woods. Grandma takes one of my elbows; Trullia takes the other. They are human crutches, supporting my weight as I hobble between trees in the direction of the campfire.

Finally, there's the orange campfire light flickering through the night. The police have Mike and Charlie and Gus in handcuffs, and Henry Jack is talking to the cops, his face even more furrowed than ever in the glow of the fire.

His face lights up when he sees me.

"Holy showman!" he says. "I was worried about you."

"*I* was worried about *you*."

"Guess that means you two are friends," says one of the police officers.

Henry Jack and I both nod.

"What the heck were you doing here, with Queenie Grace?" demands Trullia.

Henry Jack waves a hand.

"Long story," he responds. "Tell you later."

"I didn't do anything, Trullia," Mike calls.

"Likely story," Grandma retorts. "That would be why you're in handcuffs?"

"The kid jumped on me! Charlie had to hold him in self-defense!" Mike insists, his face scrunched up.

"Yeah, right," I retort, the handcuffs around Mike's wrists making me brave.

"Why don't you tell everybody what you three were doing here in the woods?" I say to Mike, my elbows still held by my mother and grandmother. "You had plans to steal Queenie Grace! To sell her and make money!"

Mike just shakes his head. Gus kicks at sticks and Charlie scratches his beard on his shoulder.

"Darn kid should go back to West Virginia where she belongs," mutters Mike.

Trullia drops my elbow.

"You will *not* talk to my daughter that way!" she shouts, stepping close to Mike's face. "I have half a mind to just slap your face!"

"Ma'am," says one of the officers, "calm down."

"I told you that man was no good," Grandma mumbles, still holding my right elbow.

"And that darn elephant needs to go," Charlie says. "It had Gus pinned on the ground! Just held him down with her hoof and kept him there!"

"Queenie Grace was protecting us!" I say.

"Oh, and that's why she tried to crush a man," Mike spat.

"If she wanted to crush him, he'd be flat as a pancake!" Trullia says.

The police start asking questions about Queenie Grace: *How old is she? Who's her legal owner? Has she ever hurt someone?*

Grandma, small and steady, answers all their questions. She's calm until she starts talking about Grandpa Bill and how he just died, and then she dissolves into crying.

Tears fill my eyes, too. My ankle aches and so does my heart. I'm so tired, so scared. The police ask for the address, for Grandma's address, for the location of the elephant.

I swear I hear Grandpa's scratchy voice inside my head, saying, *Save Queenie Grace. Take good care of my girl.*

"Grandma," I say, "can we go back now, before they get to

Queenie Grace? I'm afraid they're going to take her away."

Grandma hugs me. "I'm afraid, too, Lily."

We get back in the car and the police are still in the woods, talking to the three handcuffed men and to Henry Jack and Faith. She showed up while the bad guys were being put in handcuffs.

Grandma Violet drives, fast and furious, and we ride in silence. When we get back to Grandma's place, I say, "May I have some alone time with Queenie Grace?"

"Of course, honey," Grandma says.

Grandma and Trullia go inside, and I go to Queenie Grace.

"I'm really sorry," I say to her, reaching out and touching the skin of her trunk. "It was a bad idea, that running-away thing. It might have made things worse. But at least the bad guys can't get you now. That's one good thing, right?"

The elephant snuffles. My ankle hurts and so I lie down, on my back, under the stars. I keep talking, looking up at Queenie Grace.

"So I'm sorry if me being here caused any problems for you. I never meant for that to happen. I've really started to like you . . . to *love* you, Queenie Grace."

I can see her eyes shining watery in the light of the moon. Queenie Grace lowers herself slowly to the ground. She lies right next to me, just like she did that time when I was little, when I fell off my bike. This time, though, I have no fear. All

I feel is comfort, and love.

The swishing tail, flappy ears, bristly rough hairs, the snuffling sounds of her breath, the swinging trunk. We lie side by side, Queenie Grace and me. It's a universe of elephant.

Except now, I'm not afraid. Now I can feel the heat of Queenie Grace and I can hear her breathing and I feel no fear. Nothing but love here. The universe of elephant has become my world.

I cuddle up to her.

"Queenie Grace," I say. "You are one amazing elephant."

Queenie Grace Is Taken Away

Oh no. They are taking me away.

I tried to save my friends. The bad men are the ones who need to be taken away.

Violet takes off my howdah, unloads the backpacks. Police officers are telling her that she can make a choice: let them decide where I go, or she can make a choice.

"The sanctuary in Tampa," she says in between weeping.

Lily and Henry Jack are sobbing, too. Even the officers look sad.

"We are just doing our job, ma'am," one of them says to Violet. He pats her awkwardly on the back. "The elephant could be dangerous. After all, she did pin a man to the ground."

I am not dangerous!

Trullia goes inside, slams the door.

"What's going on?" calls Mary across the yard.

Nobody answers. They are crying too hard.

If Bill were here, he would tell them. If Bill were here, everything would be okay.

Easier to Ask What's *Right*

The emergency room swirls with people and problems. Somebody gags and throws up; somebody else mutters something about how the world is ending. It smells horrible in here, and the air-conditioning is way too cold.

I slump, exhausted beyond belief, wheezing, ankle throbbing, with Trullia sitting beside me and going on and on and on and on about how dangerous it was to run away with an elephant and how I need to think before I act. I want to put my hands over my ears, but that would be super disrespectful, so I just sit here and bite the inside of my lip. *Keep it inside.* I'm feeling as if I might die from grief: from both the missing of my grandpa and the missing of Queenie Grace. They took her away.

"Her color looks off," says a lady next to me.

"It's just that she can't breathe," says Trullia. "She tried to run away tonight. With an elephant, no less."

"Oh my," says the lady.

It's nearly three o'clock in the morning when they finally call me back into a hospital room. I have to change into a gown—one of those stupid embarrassing open-in-the-back gowns—and I have to have some tests and receive some breathing treatments and some medicine. They x-ray my ankle; it's only a sprain. It's five a.m. when we finally get to leave the ER.

"Did you call Dad?" I ask Trullia as we get in her car.

"No," she says. "He doesn't need to know."

I take out my phone and I text: Asthma attack. Was in hosp. but OK now. Also twisted ankle.

Within a minute, Dad texts back.

R u OK????!!

Yes. Love you.

Love you, too!

Trullia drives like she's mad, all fast and yanking the wheel and slamming on the brakes. She hums, but it's an angry and frustrated hum, like she's trying to keep curse words inside.

"What's wrong?" I ask. As if I don't know.

"I have to help Faith at trapeze school in less than two hours," she says. "It's the holidays—the freaking holidays!— and my father just died and he's barely in the ground when my daughter takes off with an elephant and a neighbor boy. I keep getting phone calls that things have gone wrong, things are changing left and right, and I haven't slept and I haven't eaten. I need a cigarette. I need to sleep. My boyfriend—my *ex*-boyfriend—is probably going to jail! And you want to know what's wrong? Wouldn't it be easier to ask what's *right*?"

I think about saying *I'm sorry*, but that wouldn't change anything. Trullia stares straight ahead, driving fast and furious.

"Please get Queenie Grace back," I say. "Don't let them keep her. She didn't do anything wrong. Nothing at all. She's just sad, that's all. Plus, she saved us from those guys. She was defending the people she loves."

"Not one more word," Trullia says, her voice as hard as chains. "Not one more word about the elephant or anything else. Not. One. More. Word."

Fine.

I slump down in the seat, cross my arms. I'm not wearing my seat belt, but she doesn't even bring it up. Of course not.

I give up. I will never have a mom who takes me to the hospital without complaining, and I will never have a mom who tells me to buckle up because she loves me.

She'll never explain why she left and she'll never think she might come back and she'll never ever in a million years say those words: *I love you.*

Not even on a night when I might have died.

I just close my eyes, and all I can see is the silhouette of Queenie Grace, and I wonder where she might be at this very minute, what she might be doing right now. I wish I'd never started to care about her. I wish I was still afraid, that I still didn't trust her not to hurt me, that I never started loving Queenie Grace.

That would be so much easier.

Queenie Grace Feels Fear
in Her Bones

I am afraid. They are taking me away. That is what they say, these men with eyes like stones.

I feel fear in my bones. I don't know where I will go. They say "Tampa," but I do not know what that means. I only know that it is not home.

A large truck is on the road. There is a trailer. I am loaded. I am chained. Chained. Again.

Nobody Ever Owns an Elephant

My grandmother has been up pacing all night long, she says when we get home. It is early Saturday morning.

"I've been worried sick!" she exclaims. Grandma's face is the exact opposite of the smiling SpongeBob face on her yellow nightshirt. She hasn't brushed her hair, and it's a tangle of white and purple.

"Why didn't you call me to let me know that Lily was okay?" she asks Trullia.

"Forgot," Trullia says. "I'm going to bed. And I'm going to bed in *my* room. I'm tired of sleeping on the sofa, and I'm tired of trying to answer questions, and I'm tired of trying to please somebody who can never be pleased."

"And that would be me?" my grandmother demands.

"That would be *everybody*," she says. "Every body. Every

single human being in this whole stinking world. Especially Mike."

The door to the bedroom slams. We hear the creak of the bed, extra loud, as if she threw herself down on it. My grandmother looks at me.

"I'm sorry, Lily. She can be difficult. Very, very difficult. Believe me, I know."

"I guess she's tired, like super tired. Stressed, too, I guess."

"Don't make excuses for her, honey," says my grandmother. "She needs to face her own mistakes."

I'm sleeping on the sofa when the phone rings, jolting me from a dream. For a minute, I'm confused and can't quite figure out where I am or what time of the day it might be. Then I remember: *last night, this morning*. I hear my grandmother talking, and I just lie there, staring up at an old picture of my dad and Trullia. It's hard to believe that they were young and in love, once upon a time.

"Oh," Grandma says, her voice soft and sad. "Well, thank you for letting us know. We will indeed miss her terribly. She was with my husband for years, and he just passed. That may be why she's been acting out, from the grief. She was always very good, up until now. And believe me, I never wanted it to come to this. But finances are tight, plus we can't have her circus act without my husband. And of course, the incident last night with the police."

I sit up, rub my eyes, and try to listen harder. Poor Queenie Grace.

"Well, she has been stressed, very much so," says my grandmother's voice from the kitchen. "And I'm sure she's quite exhausted today, after last night. It was quite a night."

"Queenie Grace isn't feeling so well," Grandma says when she hangs up. "That was the sanctuary."

My heart falls.

"What's wrong?"

"She's sick and she's sad and she won't eat," Grandma replies. I feel dizzy, as if I might throw up. If anything happens to Queenie Grace, it's mostly my fault. I should have known better than to run away with her and Henry Jack. I knew it wasn't a good plan.

"I hope they're being nice to her there," I say.

"Oh, they'll be very nice to her. Pamper her. She'll have lots of room to run, plus other elephants live there."

"Can . . . can we see her? Visit?"

"Of course, Lily, honey. She's been part of our lives for a very long time. In fact, she's family. The elephant is family, and family stays in one another's lives, even when bad things happen. Even when they have to live separate lives, in separate places, they're still family."

It's the middle of the morning, and I assume that Trullia is skipping today at the trapeze school. She looks pretty rough: her hair all messed up and smudged makeup under her eyes. She's wearing the same clothes from last night, and actually, so am I. Sometimes you're just too tired to change.

I'm sitting at the kitchen table, still trying to wake up, painting a picture of Queenie Grace in sorrowful shades of gray. My grandmother is on the sofa, posed beneath the painting I did of Grandpa. Trullia's twisted up in the recliner, legs curled under her.

"So a friend just texted me," my mother says, peering at her phone. "He says that we have an offer from someone who wants to buy Queenie Grace."

"She's in a good place," Grandma says. "The matter is closed."

"But we could use the money," Trullia continues. Grandma ignores her. I guess she's had a lot of practice at that through the years.

Trullia keeps right on talking to herself. "But now that she's at the sanctuary, who owns her: us or them?"

Nobody ever owns an elephant, I think. *Just like nobody ever really owns a human being.*

Trullia just won't give it up. She talks and talks, despite the fact that Grandma isn't answering, all about how they can really use the cash.

"I don't care about the money!" Grandma yells. "I care about Queenie Grace! She provided for us for years, and it's time she has a nice retirement."

"But that kind of money could pay for the funeral, Mom," Trullia says.

"They'll get their money when they get it!" Grandma replies. "Let's just stop talking about it, Trullia. Please. I am so exhausted. I'm tired and I'm sad and I'm filled with regret. I'm already missing Queenie Grace. I feel terrible for letting her go. So glad that Bill doesn't know what is going on. He'd have a conniption fit."

"I never thought I'd say this," Trullia says, "but it's actually good that Dad's not here. This would break his heart into a zillion pieces. And that's something I'd never want to see."

Grandma sighs. She's sniffling.

I just keep on painting in shades of gray.

Queenie Grace Is Sick

I refuse to move from the trailer. I want to go home. I do not want to go into that place, even though I can smell and hear that other elephants are here.

I will not eat. I will not drink. The men are frustrated. One of them calls Violet on his phone. I listen to him talk. I hear Violet's voice. Oh, how I miss my home.

I did nothing wrong.

I Never Should Have Come

It's nine o'clock Saturday night and a TV news van—Channel 8—is parked next door. The reporter holds a microphone to Fire-Eating Charlie's mouth.

"I'm glad it's gone," he says. "That elephant could have killed somebody."

"No," I whisper. "Queenie Grace wouldn't hurt a flea."

Mary the Bearded Lady comes outside, and the microphone moves to her.

"I liked that elephant," she says. "And I'm sorry that she's gone. You should interview little Lily over there. . . ."

She points at me.

"She's related to the elephant," Mary says. "Queenie Grace has been with Lily's grandfather for a long time."

The reporter, a snazzy slick woman in a business suit and

heels, bustles briskly across the yard. A guy hoisting a TV camera follows. The reporter comes up to me, shoves the microphone in my face.

"What's your name?" she asks. Her lipstick gleams bright red.

"Lily," I say. "Lily Rose Pruitt."

"How old are you?" the lady asks.

"Twelve." I blink. The lights are blinding me.

"Do you live here?

"No, I'm just visiting. I live in West Virginia. I came for my grandpa's . . . funeral."

"And what do you think of the elephant?"

"I love her," I say.

"Do you wish you could get her back?" asks the lady.

I just nod. I can't say much, because I'm swallowing tears. There's no way I want to cry on TV.

"Are you glad you came? Do you like it here, in Gibtown?"

I just shrug.

In a way, I'm glad I came. I learned to love an elephant, and I made a new best friend who's really cool. I got to spend some time with my grandma, and I figured out that Trullia will never change. But in a bigger way, I'm all weighted down with guilt.

I never should have come here. I never should have come. I should have just stayed home where I belong, and none of this ever would have happened.

Queenie Grace Is Lost

I try to hear Bill's voice, to see his face inside my mind, but I can't. It's silent, empty.

I cannot see the stars from where I stand, but I know that the sky is dark.

Nothing Left

I head inside to the kitchen table, where my painting of Queenie Grace is lying out to dry. I pick it up and rip, rip, rip until it is gone. There is nothing left, nothing but shreds, and I drop them in the trash.

Trullia and Grandma are watching TV, loud, obviously trying to block out everything. Shame on them. They *should* be sorry and chock-full of remorse.

Thunder rumbles; lightning flashes and snaps. I gaze through the kitchen window. Rain pours. The TV people leave in a flurry of activity, and finally, there's just the silence of nighttime. A gloomy wet darkness without the shape of Queenie Grace in it.

I feel as though I could throw up. I open the door to get some fresh air. The rain has slowed down; clusters of stars are out. One group looks like an elephant swinging its trunk.

I run. I just take a step out to breathe in some new air and then, without a second thought, I launch into running full speed ahead. I run and run, tears gushing down my cheeks, through the empty and quiet trailer park, not caring what anybody thinks or says or does.

I dart past the abandoned cotton candy stand, past the old carousel, past the still Ferris wheel. I run with the attitude of someone who has just given up, who doesn't give a hoot about anything anymore. I don't even care that I'm starting to wheeze.

With every thud of my sneakers against road, I'm thinking the same thing, over and over and over: *Queenie Grace, Queenie Grace, Queenie Grace, Queenie Grace.*

I run and run until I am so tired and out of breath that I feel dead. But then I decide that I need to go back to my grandmother's.

I double over, panting. My hair is soaked; so are my clothes. I shiver. I turn around and head back.

Near my grandmother's trailer, I hear the sounds of crying. Somebody weeps from deep inside.

I stop for a minute, listen, take some slow and hesitant steps in the direction of the sobs. And then I see that somebody is hunched over in the middle of my grandmother's yard, in the spot where Queenie Grace sometimes lay. It is Trullia Lee Pruitt, collapsed on her knees in the wet grass, head in her hands, crying like crazy.

I walk up to her, reach out to touch her shoulder, pull my hand back before it makes contact.

Trullia looks up at me, tears flooding her face. The dam inside Trullia Lee Pruitt seems to be broken, and the insides spill out in a flood of grief.

"My dad's gone," she weeps. "My dad's gone and so is Queenie Grace, and Mike is a jerk. Nothing ever goes right for me. I hate my life."

I look at my mother's face, and it droops so sad and old and forlorn in the darkness, like a flower that's lost its bloom.

"Mike never cared about me," she says. "All he cares about is money. Money and the stuff you can buy with it. I'm so glad that I told him to beat it. To get lost and never come back. How could I have been so dumb? I miss my dad. I miss him so much."

"I'm sorry," I say. "I know how it feels to lose somebody. And not just somebody who died. Somebody who's still alive."

She looks up at me.

"You're too young to know that," she says.

"But I do."

She's shaking like crazy, and she looks up at me with this

wounded expression that makes my heart hurt for her, but even more for me. And that's when I explode into mad.

"You have no idea how it feels to be me," I snap, looking her straight in the eyes. Finally speaking my mind, I say steady and strong, "I used to wish you were dead. I actually used to wish you died, because that might be better than knowing that you didn't want me."

Trullia flinches.

"I was only three! I didn't even do anything wrong, and you left. Left, just like that! Who does that? What kind of a mother leaves her baby? If not for Dad, I'd go crazy from the wondering and the loneliness of not having my mother. Do you know how it feels to be the only kid at school who doesn't have a mother?"

Trullia clenches fistfuls of her hair in each hand, pulling it, the insides of her arms pressed against her ears like she's having a tantrum. *No,* I think. *You won't drown me out. You need to hear me.*

"So what was it?" I demand, loud. "Was I too fussy for you? Too much work? Did I drive you crazy with my whining, or my crying, or my asthma?"

She shakes her head.

I stamp my foot in the soaked-through and beaten-down grass.

"Plus that time I was so scared! That time I was riding my bike and you weren't looking and I fell and wrecked!

Remember? Queenie Grace lay down beside me. She almost squished me, crushed me to death! I actually thought I was going to die!"

"Lily," Trullia says, "Queenie Grace wasn't trying to hurt you. She was trying to help you."

"YOU WERE THE ONE WHO SHOULD HAVE BEEN HELPING ME!" I scream.

"I know," Trullia says. "I do know that."

"And I never could understand why you did the things you did. Like run away. Like leave me and Dad. Like you didn't come visit. All that."

Trullia struggles to stand. She shakes her head.

"Let's go inside," she says. "There's no real excuse for what I did, but maybe I can try to explain."

One of the Best Nights of
Queenie Grace's Life

I trail after the men. I follow their lead, and I see other elephants watching. Some peer from the trees; others from a
big barn.

There wafts a smell that I remember. An elephant never
forgets, and I remember this scent. It is the smell of my baby!
The smell of Little Gray!

I stop; I sway.

And then she thunders running, bursting from out of the
barn, as fast as an elephant can run. Her feet thud; I feel the
earth shake. My body quakes, and I take a shaky step.

It is my baby! It is Little Gray! She is all grown up, taller
than me, and she recognizes that I am her mother. She
remembers. Little Gray never forgets, either!

I trumpet, loud.

Little Gray, my baby, my baby, my baby! Little Gray, Little Gray, Little Gray!

Oh, how I've missed my beautiful child, my little one now grown so big.

Little Gray runs to me. She lifts her trunk, I lift mine, and we hug with our two trunks. This is one of the best nights of my life.

I am filled with light.

Family Needs to Be Together on Nights Like This

Trullia and I trudge inside. Grandma sips a cup of hot tea, blowing on it to cool it off. Her small bare feet are propped up in the recliner.

"Look at the kitchen table, Lily," Grandma says.

I do, and there's my painting of Queenie Grace, taped back together. It's not a perfect tape job and doesn't exactly match up just right, but Grandma Violet was able to dig all the pieces from the trash can.

"You put it back together," I say. "I can't believe you found all the pieces."

"You can put anything back together, if you want it badly enough, and I want that painting," Grandma says. "Never throw away your art. Your art is part of you."

I just shrug.

"Come sit with me, Lily," she says, and pats her lap. "Family needs to be together on these kind of nights."

Grandma releases the recliner and I perch on her tiny lap.

"Is Queenie Grace doing okay?" I ask, and my grandmother circles me with her arms.

"Nobody answered the phone," she says. "I tried to find out, but nobody answered. I guess we will have to wait until morning."

I sigh. Night is too long, and morning seems like a lifetime away.

"So," Trullia says, sinking down into the other chair. "I have some things to say." She takes out a cigarette, but then remembers and puts it away.

My grandmother sips her tea, carefully, behind me.

"So," Trullia says, "I left, and I never should have done it like that. I should have maybe tried some counseling, or at least taken you with me, but I just up and left. If I could take it back I would, but it's like a breath: here and gone. No getting it back again. I think that maybe I was depressed and I had lots of problems, and I didn't even know what the heck I was thinking or feeling. And that's why I just kind of left you alone with your dad, because I knew he could take care of you. I knew he *would* take care of you."

She blows out a breath like she's smoking. Grandma

jiggles her knees beneath me, as if she's trying to soothe a fussy baby. Or maybe she's just nervous.

"And so I know I was wrong. Your father did nothing wrong. It was just that I was young and dumb and didn't know what I wanted. I wasn't ready to be a mother, and I wouldn't have been a good one, Lily. It was for the best that I left."

My grandmother nods.

"She was a mess when she came to us, honey. Needed medication and needed a place to rest. We never judged her, or blamed her. Nobody really knew what exactly was wrong, or how to fix it. We just tried to help her get better, but we never, ever said that she'd made a good choice. We just loved her, and that's all we could do. We all do our best with what we have at the time."

I nod, look down at my legs.

"Queenie Grace helped her a lot," says my grandmother. "It was as if Queenie Grace knew that Trullia had some problems, and she just loved her, too. Accepted her without reservations or judgment. Why, Queenie Grace might have even saved our daughter's life."

"She did," Trullia says. "And I didn't always show it, but I loved her, too. I always loved her. I still love her."

"So it was just . . . you?" I ask Trullia. "Just that you weren't . . . right?"

Trullia nods, sad and slow.

"I wasn't well," she says. "I wouldn't have been able to take good care of you, not at that time."

Grandma puts her tea down on the end table.

"Are you okay now?" I ask Trullia. "Did you get . . . better?"

She ekes out a small, tight smile.

"Lily," she says, "I am so much better, especially now that you're here. I know that I seem mean sometimes, that I seem to not care. But it's probably my illness making me that way, not that I'm trying to make excuses. Really, I do care. I just don't know how to show it, so sometimes it might seem like I'm being a jerk. And every day—every single minute of every single day—is still a struggle for me."

"Trullia," says Grandma behind me, "I think that you're making excuses. It was just that you weren't ready to be a mother, and you would not have been a good one. You were very immature."

"You're right, Mom," Trullia admits. "And, Lily, I'm sorry. I am so . . . very sorry."

She looks at me, and her eyes' light is blue and so clear, and I know that she's being honest and true. I know just what to do.

And then I make the first move: I stand up and go to Trullia and I draw her into a big strong hug that feels a lot like forgiveness. She hugs me back, shaking. I wrap her in my arms as if I'm the grown-up. It makes me feel strong. This feels like hope and faith, faith that things really will be okay.

"It'll be all right," I say. "Trullia, it'll be okay. I promise."

I still can't quite bring myself to call her "Mom." I just can't. But this, tonight, it's a start.

We Will Never Let Go Again

Oh, how much I've missed being a mother. I love nuzzling with Little Gray. The men here laugh; they take pictures; they rave about miracles and magic.

Finally, the men leave and it is nobody but us: Little Gray and Queenie Grace. I can see the love on her face, and her eyes won't leave mine. They shine.

We will never let go again.

No More Bad News

The phone rings, jolting all three of us. I'm hoping for no bad news, no more bad news, please, no bad news tonight.

My grandmother's eyebrows lift as she listens. Her cheeks make apples in her face. She holds one hand to her heart.

"Yes?" she says. "Oh my goodness! Oh, I can't even believe that!"

Trullia and I watch her, mouthing the word "What?"

My grandmother holds up a finger. Her face shines.

"How did you know?" she asks, then listens with shimmering eyes, nodding.

"Okay," she finally says. "Oh, this is wonderful. Thank you so much for letting me know."

I look at Trullia.

"What?" she says to Grandma. "What happened?"

Grandma holds up her index finger again. She looks as if she wants to kiss the phone.

"Thank you," she says. "I swear, this is the best news ever."

Grandma hangs up. She beams, and her face looks as if it's going to explode with gladness.

"The suspense is killing us," says my mother.

"What?" I ask. "We're dying here."

My grandmother just smiles, so big. Her eyes shine full of light, and she does her little dance move with jazz hands.

"Queenie Grace is just fine," she says. "Actually, she's great. They finally got her to move out of the trailer, and you will not believe what happened."

Grandma actually bounces with excitement.

"What? What?"

My grandmother's eyes brim.

"When Queenie Grace finally decided to leave the trailer, there was another elephant who came running so fast," Grandma says. "Queenie Grace and this elephant obviously knew and loved each other, they say, and they went crazy with joy. They say you can always tell by the behavior and the reactions, even if the elephants met many years ago. And there's a certain way that mother elephants act with their young. . . ."

I catch my breath, and Grandma puts her arm around me.

"Queenie Grace had a baby," she says, "many years ago. The elephant experts think that this other elephant may be that baby."

"Wow," Trullia says. She runs both hands through her hair. "Wow!"

I don't even know what to say. I'm so thrilled for Queenie Grace. And for the one that they think is her baby, because every baby deserves a mom who loves it.

"So . . . now what?" asks Trullia.

"Well, Queenie Grace will be staying there with her baby," states Grandma. "Forever. Nobody will ever separate them again."

"Oh," I say, "I wish I could meet the baby. And say goodbye to Queenie Grace."

"You will, honey," Grandma Violet says. "I already thought of that. We'll go see them before your flight home."

My heart lifts like wings. I'm so happy I could fly.

Queenie Grace and Little Gray
Are Staying Together

Little Gray and I are going to stay together! They say that this nice place of elephants is now our home, and that the people we love will visit a lot. They will visit soon.

Little Gray and I stand side by side, touching always, never letting go. We are staying together . . . forever. I can't wait for her to meet my family . . . *our* family.

Flying and Hugging a Lion

It's Sunday, the morning of New Year's Eve, and I have to wait until tomorrow to see Queenie Grace and her baby.

"I can't wait!" I say to Grandma and Trullia. "Today's going to go so slow. I can't wait until tomorrow."

"You know what they say: Patience is a virtue," Grandma says, making air quotes. She's frying eggs, wearing her SpongeBob nightshirt.

"Well, I have an offer from Faith that will help you pass the time," says Trullia. "She wants you to come to trapeze school today. She wants to teach you trapeze. Free. She's a better teacher than me, much more patient."

"Uh, cool? But . . . what if I can't? What if I'm afraid?"

"You'll be fine," says Trullia with a grin. "Just throw your heart over the bar and your body will follow."

So here I am: in a majestic red tent all set up for teaching trapeze. "Trapeze arts," as Faith says. Faith shimmers in a glittery silver costume, and Henry Jack is here, too.

"Why didn't you come over last night?" I ask him. "You missed all the TV people."

"What do you think I am, crazy?" replies Henry Jack. "I'm in the public eye enough. I didn't want to be on TV. No way."

I laugh, punch him lightly in the arm.

"Coward," I say.

"Who's the one afraid of everything?" asks Henry Jack.

"Not me," I say, as Faith hands me a costume in my size. It's glittery green, like Magic Mountain in summer, like Henry Jack's eyes.

"I'm not afraid," I say, feeling the cool green of the sequined costume. "I'm not afraid anymore."

So I change into my costume, feeling a little silly in the outfit.

"You're gorgeous, Lily!" Faith says when I come out of the cramped dressing room.

"Yeah," Henry Jack agrees. "You look pretty cool. Like you actually maybe know what you're doing on the trapeze."

"No clue," I say. "That's why we have Faith."

First thing we do is called ground school. Faith teaches

me all about how to stretch, the importance of listening to her for commands, how and when to tuck my knees.

"Now for your safety belt," Faith says, cinching me tight into a harness thing.

"Ow," I say. "It's tight."

"Believe me," says Faith, "you don't want a loose belt when you're dangling up there in space."

I look up at the bar, the trapeze, the ceiling of the high tent. My heart skitters.

"Okay," I say. "I guess you're right."

Faith brings out a piece of wood.

"This is the same size as the platform up there," she says. "You're going to practice with 'Ready' and 'Hup!' Once you've got that down pat, you'll practice pulling your knees through that low trapeze."

Faith points to a trapeze not much higher than me.

"Don't worry," she says. "It gets easier when you're high up. The force of the swing makes it simpler to get your knees through. Then next thing you know, you'll be flying!"

An hour later, Faith still has me practicing climbing the ladder and doing this routine again and again. I know it by heart:

Swing out. Tuck knees, swing from trapeze. Let go of the bar with my hands. Look back with hands out, like waiting to be caught. Grab the bar; take off my knees. Keep legs straight

behind. Quickly move forward, back, forward! Tuck knees;
release! Fall into the net.

"The net will always catch you," says Faith. "It's all about
trust."

Later Faith says I'm ready for catch school.

"Um, what's that?" I ask as Henry Jack grins and pumps
his fist.

"That's where I fly on that trapeze, and you fly on that
one," Faith explains.

Faith points to the bars on either end of the tent, the wire
stretched between them. This quivery wire looks way too
thin, the bars not strong. My heart thuds.

"You'll fly, I'll fly, we'll meet in the middle, and you'll let
go. You'll just trust me and let go, and I'll catch you."

"Uh, but what if you don't?" The world inside the tent
spins dizzy.

"I'll catch you," says silvery Faith with a big smile. "But
don't forget, there's the net. There's always the net."

I climb the ladder, step onto the platform. Breathe. Take a
big breath, breathe again. I reach out and grab the bar, put
my body over the lower bar. *I throw my heart over the bar
and my body follows, just like Trullia says.*

Another breath, a glance down at Henry Jack. Faith yells,
"Ready! Go!"

And so I do. I go. I fly. I let go with my hands and I reach out for Faith. She catches me and we swing, flying high. My stomach is in my head; my head is in the sky; my heart swoops.

I am flying.

And as I fly, I catch a glimpse of someone who has come into the tent to watch. It's my mother, her face lit up with pride.

"You did great," Henry Jack says as we walk back toward Grandma's house after my trapeze lessons. "You weren't even scared."

"I was, just a little bit. But I tried to fight it."

Henry Jack nods, flipping back his hair.

"That's all it takes sometimes," he says.

George is walking toward us, all jaunty in his blue jeans and beret.

"Hey, kiddos!" he calls.

"Hey, George," Henry Jack and I answer in unison. We all stop and give one another high fives. Except for George and us, it's more of a low five.

"What are you two up to?"

"Oh, just passing time until we go see Queenie Grace and her baby," I say. "I learned to fly! Henry Jack's mom gave me trapeze lessons."

"Fabulous," George says. "I'm just heading home to take

care of Boldo and give him his medicine. Hey, why don't you guys stop by? Old Boldo loves company, and he especially loves the young'uns."

"Sure," says Henry Jack, while I hesitate.

"Um, I'm kind of scared of lions," I say.

George smiles.

"Boldo will fix that," he says.

I think for a minute. I need to be brave, to push past my fear. And, what the heck, I've already learned to fly today!

"Okay," I say. "Let's go."

And so I'm in George's tiny trailer, petting an enormous lazy lion. Boldo has green and yellow eyes and soft fur, and he moves his head like a gigantic cat as I scratch him behind his ears. He looks hypnotized, so relaxed, and that makes me relax, too.

"He's really sweet," I say, as Boldo gazes up at me and presses his huge head to my chest. His fur feels like my favorite winter coat.

"Of course he's sweet," says George. "He's my baby."

"I didn't know wild lions could be this tame," I say.

"If you work with them and give them love," he replies, "they will give you love in return."

"How old is he?"

"Too old. He may not have much longer," George replies, his eyes sad. George reaches out and strokes Boldo's head.

"Awwwww. He's so nice. It's not fair," I say.

"But he's had a great life," George says. "He's loved and been loved, and isn't that all that any of us could want, before we leave this earth behind?"

"Yep," says Henry Jack, "my brother was really loved, too. And he loved us."

I swallow hard. I feel so bad that Henry Jack lost his twin.

"You get it, kid," says George. "Life is short, ya know? So you just gotta go for it. Seize the day! Leap for joy! Eat ice cream!"

Boldo is making this contented growly purr, rubbing his head against me.

"Want a Boldo hug?" George says to me.

I don't even have to think about it.

"Sure," I say.

"Stand up. Get ready for the best hug of your life."

I pull away from Boldo and stand up. The lion does, too.

"Hug," George says to the lion. "Hug Lily."

And he does. Boldo the lion jumps up and puts his front paws on my shoulders; I fall back a little from his weight, and George supports me from behind. And then Boldo pulls me into the softest, furriest, best hug ever. It's tight and fluffy and Boldo is huge, full of power and wildness, but I'm not one bit scared.

I hug him back.

Queenie Grace's New Year's Eve

I know that this night is New Year's Eve, and I know that some people like to make a big deal. I used to like how Bill went outside at midnight and yelled at the sky. "Happy New Year!" he'd shout. "May all good things come to us this year!"

All good things have already come to me. I raise my eyes to the sky, and I send a silent thank-you to my *mahout*. I do believe that Bill had something to do with this reunion, even though we can no longer see him.

Bill the Giant still works his magic.

New Year's Eve

New Year's Eve, and Grandma has pointy hats and noise-makers and big silly red glasses with the numbers of the new year.

"And we'll do a toast to the brand-new year at midnight," Grandma says. She has plastic champagne glasses and sparkling grape juice already set out on the kitchen table. "Bill used to go outside and yell at the sky. Maybe we'll do that, too."

Finally, it's midnight. We strap on the cardboard hats and we wear the crazy glasses and we blow the noisemakers. Grandma and Trullia and Henry Jack and me: it's our own private little party.

"May the new year bring better things and many blessings," Grandma says as we all lift our plastic glasses in a toast.

"Cheers," Trullia says. "To good news! To mother-daughter reunions! To elephant-daughter reunions!"

We clink our plastic glasses and drink the carbonated grape juice. And then, at five minutes past midnight, Henry Jack and I go outside.

"May all good things come to us this year!" I shout at the sky, looking up.

A few neighbors are doing fireworks, and the sky lights up with color and explosions.

"Isn't it against the law to do those on your own?" I ask.

Henry Jack laughs.

"Yeah," he says. "But nobody in Gibtown really cares, obviously."

Mary the Bearded Lady is outside, holding a single sparkler. It lights her face, her beard bushy in the glow.

"Happy New Year's, Mary!" Henry Jack calls, and she walks over to where the two yards meet.

"Happy New Year's to you," she says. The sparkler sizzles and then fizzles out, going dark. She places it on the ground.

"It's hot," she says. "Don't touch it."

"I know," Henry Jack says. "My mom and I do these all the time, for special celebrations."

"Well," says Mary, "I don't feel like there's too much to celebrate right now, but sometimes you just have to make half an effort. Because what else can you do?"

"Some good news is that Queenie Grace found a baby

she had years ago," I say. "I guess you've heard."

Mary nods. She tries to smile.

"I heard. It's all over Gibtown," she says. "I'm happy for them. They deserve that."

"We're going to see them tomorrow," Henry Jack says. "The sanctuary wanted us to give it a day for them to get reacquainted and reunite in private."

"We can't wait to see them," I say. "That'll be a great way to start the new year."

Mary nods, sighs.

"Yeah," she says. "I don't know how my new year's going to go. With Charlie gone and all. He just up and left, after that arrest. Him and Mike both. I've never been alone before, so this is all new to me."

Henry Jack and I say nothing. The fireworks have stopped; the sky is silent.

"Sometimes life brings surprises," says Mary. "Not all of them good."

I step closer to Mary the Bearded Lady. Her voice and face seem brave, but her eyes brim with sorrow.

"I'm sorry," I say. "I'm sorry about your husband leaving."

Inside, I'm thinking, *You're better off without that horrible man, and so are your dogs.*

But I don't say that. Instead, I just reach over with both arms and embrace Mary.

The three little dogs push open the screen door and

bound joyfully into the yard. They are not wearing tutus.

Mary hugs me back, and I can feel both the appreciation and the grief in her large and soft body.

"I don't know if I'll ever let him come back here," she mumbles, "but I'll forgive. I'll have to forgive him or it'll just eat me up on the inside."

I nod. I know all about that.

Looking Up

We see fireworks in the nighttime: Little Gray and I. The bursts of light and noise symbolize celebration and new beginnings and hope.

We both raise our eyes to the sky. Sometimes looking up is the best thing you can do.

Room to Roam

On Monday morning, the first day of the brand-new year, we pile in the car for the drive to the elephant sanctuary: Trullia, Grandma, Henry Jack, and me. We're all bubbling with excitement, even Trullia.

It's a short drive north, just ten miles, and we can hardly contain our smiles. We sing along with the radio, all of us car-dancing, the windows open and blowing our hair.

And finally . . . there it is. Looming like Oz.

"Oh," breathes Grandma Violet when we see the sign: *Room to Roam Elephant Sanctuary.*

We get out of the car, walking all full of wonder and discovery, like Dorothy and the Scarecrow and the Tin Man and the Cowardly Lion. I guess I'm Dorothy. Grandma's the Lion, searching for the courage to be alone without Grandpa

Bill. Henry Jack is the Scarecrow, but he already has a great brain behind that wrinkled face. And Trullia? Well, she'd be the Tin Man . . . maybe getting her heart. Finally.

"We're off to see the elephants," I sing to the tune from the *Wizard of Oz* movie. "The wonderful elephants of Us. Queenie Grace and Baby."

Grandma and Trullia and Henry Jack play along, and we all skip as if we're on the yellow brick road, heading for that beautiful city on the hill. Except there's no wicked witch; no flying monkeys. Not anymore. All the fear is gone.

This place is so pretty: overflowing with leafy trees, explosions of brilliant flowers, lush green grass. It smells like Florida, but mixed in with a little bit of wild. Two huge red barns, some rainbow-painted buildings, plenty of room to graze and play. Lots of open land, spreading out as far as my eyes can see, leading to the edge of blue sky. Elephants are everywhere, dotting the horizon with gray. There are a few workers washing elephants, scrubbing them with big brushes in a water area that must be the elephant bath.

"Wow," says Henry Jack. "This is like a retirement community for rich people. The best of the best. Maybe they even have their own swimming pools!"

"I bet they love it here," I say.

"Wonder where they are?" Trullia says.

"What if we can't recognize Queenie Grace?" I ask. "You know, like all the elephants look kind of alike?"

"Oh, we'll recognize her, all right," Grandma Violet says.

"And she'll definitely know us," Henry Jack adds. "She probably smells us already."

And then, in a rush of pounding gray and swinging ears, there they are! Queenie Grace and her baby: both of them close to the same size, with the same soulful eyes. They stop, side by side, and meet our gazes, ears flapping in the same rhythm.

"Queenie Grace is just a little bit smaller than her baby," Grandma Violet says.

"Just like you and me, Mom," Trullia says. "And also like Lily and me. The baby's always the tallest in this family, so it seems."

Queenie Grace and her baby lock trunks for a minute, and we all laugh and clap.

"They're hugging!" I say.

And then Queenie Grace plods straight to me, nuzzling my neck with her trunk. I kiss her on that long, searching, bristly-haired trunk. *Who would have believed I'd ever kiss an elephant?*

"Hi, Queenie Grace," I say. "Sorry for getting you in trouble the other night. We shouldn't have tried that running-away thing."

"Yeah," says Henry Jack. "I have to admit: that was a big mistake."

"It's all right." My grandmother waves her hand. "Let the

past be the past, bygones be bygones. Time to move *forward*. Plus, the big mistake somehow resulted in this good outcome."

"You're right," Henry Jack says. "This is like the bright side of that night."

"And mistakes are made to be forgiven, and forgotten," Trullia says. "Lord knows I've made enough of them in my lifetime."

Queenie Grace nudges her baby forward, as if to introduce her to us.

"Hi," I say. "Nice to meet you." I shake her trunk as if I'm shaking a human hand. "I'm Lily. My grandfather was Bill the Giant. He was Queenie Grace's—your mother's—owner. Her owner, her trainer, her *mahout*. Her favorite person in the world."

The baby looks at me. Her eyes are so sweet. She lifts her trunk and she brushes it, soft as a smooch, across my cheek.

And then Queenie Grace kneels on the ground beside me.

"Is she praying?" I ask.

"No," Grandma Violet says. "She wants to give you a ride."

I don't even have to think about it. I just scramble up onto Queenie Grace's back, helped up by Trullia and Henry Jack and Grandma and a small ladder leaning against a fence. I settle in and grasp her skin, squeezing my knees against her. Queenie Grace begins to walk, slow and steady and sure, way around the sanctuary. She goes far; it's like she's giving me a tour. And I'm not one bit afraid! It feels as if this is where I belong: sitting on top of the world, riding Queenie Grace in this peaceful place. Birds chirp, and there are the sounds of elephants. No cars; no traffic. Just quiet, and nature, and relaxation. I roll along with the rhythm of her steps.

"It's so beautiful here," I say. "I like your new home."

Queenie Grace's ears flap as if she agrees.

She walks back toward our family: Grandma and Trullia and Henry Jack and Baby. Her ears flap like happy flags; I can actually feel the celebration and contentment in her body. It's our own little parade, our own private big top. Our own "Step Right Up" moment.

"There's no place like home, right?" I say to Queenie Grace. "I'll be going home soon, too."

But I wish I were staying longer than tomorrow. I don't want to go. Not yet.

The Girl Lily Is Leaving

The girl Lily will be leaving me. She is going home. I will see her in the summertime, she says. We will always be best friends, she says. Little Gray and I will make each other happy, and we will all be together again, she says. Her words are nice, and she speaks them soft and sweet, so they do help a little bit.

I will miss this girl. She has taught me that there is always someone else to love, and to trust. Not to replace, but to grace a life with the best that person has to give.

I make noises with my crying. The others have gone to the car but Lily lingers here, with us elephants. The moon glows; stars sparkle in dark sky. My people have stayed a long time, from day into night.

"I will miss you," Lily whispers. "You're my favorite

elephant ever, in the whole wide world."

And she is my favorite girl. Henry Jack is my favorite boy. Bill the Giant was my favorite man. Little Gray is my favorite baby, no matter she big she is.

And this much I know: We will all be together again. We will. Even Bill.

In the shine from the moon and stars, I can see that Lily cries, too. Tears drip down her face, and she does not try to wipe them away. I reach out with my trunk, and I touch the tears. I taste them: salty like my own.

Lily tries to smile. Her eyes meet mine, and I try not to cry. I try, but the tears leak out.

I don't know what else to do, so I just reach out with my trunk once again, and I brush at Lily's tears. I can't make them go away, but I can at least sweep them from her face.

Lily reaches out and brushes my tears away, too.

This is all we can do.

When You Wish Upon a Star

"Look!" I say to Queenie Grace, trying to make us both stop crying. "A falling star! I need to make a wish."

Queenie Grace just looks at me funny, like I've finally lost my marbles.

"Just go with it," I say. "I think Disney started it."

I follow the star with my eyes and with my heart, just like in the movies. *What should I wish, what should I wish?*

A dozen wishes whiz through my mind as I fix my eyes on the sky. *Should I wish to be a millionaire? Nah, money wishes are the worst kind. Should I wish for my mom to come home to West Virginia? No, that's one wish that would never come true, and probably wouldn't be so great if it did.*

I finally hit upon the perfect wish, and so I wish it, hard. *I wish to stay best friends forever with Queenie Grace and her* baby and with the Alligator Boy Henry Jack, and I wish to remember forever everything I learned in Gibtown over Christmas. I wish to stay brave and to always have faith. I wish for the New Year to be happy and healthy for Grandma and Dad and me, and I even wish the same for Trullia. I wish to forgive everybody who ever hurt me, and I wish for happily ever after . . . or at least as close as it gets.

The star disappears, and Queenie Grace makes a contented little sigh like a secret in the night.

It is time for me to go, but I don't say good-bye.

"See you soon," I say. "Until we meet again, Friend."

Queenie Grace Can Feel a Secret

I can feel a secret in the air as the car full of people I love disappears into the night.

Sometimes I do sense secrets. I smell them and I see them. I smelled a secret the night that I saved Trullia's life, and I smelled secrets when I first met Mike. Charlie the Fire-Eater reeks of secrets.

And I certainly smell a secret tonight. It smells like a good one.

A Surprise

It's Tuesday, January 2, flying time. School starts again on Thursday, and then it'll be back to real life. Life in West Virginia with just Dad and me and our campground.

Early in the morning, Henry Jack stands at Grandma's door, grinning, hands hidden behind his back as the sun rises behind him.

"I have a surprise," he says. He is way too perky for this time of the day.

"What?" I ask, groggy. If you ask me, sunrise is too early for surprise. A person has to at least be able to fully open her eyes.

"Ta-da!" Henry Jack says. He holds out a tattered old red book: *Manual for Mahouts: The Care and Feeding of Elephants.*

"For you," he announces.

"What?" I say. "That's the book my grandpa gave you."

"And now I'm giving it to you, now that you're Queenie Grace's *mahout*. Little Gray's, too, I bet. It'll be 'The Amazing Queenie Grace and Little Gray and their Best Friend Lily Rose Pruitt!' Next thing you know, Lily Pruitt will be the famous Elephant Whisperer or something. Maybe you'll have your own circus troupe, be a girl on the high-flying trapeze, too. . . ."

"Keep dreaming big for me," I say, "and I'll dream big for you, too. I think you're going to do something great in your lifetime. Something ginormous, big enough for both twins."

Henry Jack blinks, pulling his feelings back inside. He flips his hair from his eyes. He hands me the book. The book smells like Grandpa Bill and like Henry Jack's house, and the pages feel old and fragile. The cover is tattered at the edges, and you can tell it's been well-loved. Well-used.

"Thanks," I say to Henry Jack as the sky turns purple and pink behind him. "I'll definitely keep this forever."

My flight is at two o'clock in the afternoon, so there's not much time left. I don't like when minutes start to tick away and there's nothing you can do to stop them or to slow them down.

Grandma's still in her nightgown. Trullia, too. Nobody has brushed their hair or their teeth; nobody has eaten. It's like we're human-sized slugs, sprawled in the living room.

"Shouldn't we, like, get moving?" I ask, and Grandma laughs.

"What's so funny about that?" I respond. "Airplanes don't wait, you know. And it's not like I can sprout wings and fly myself home."

"Guess what?" Grandma says. "I have a surprise."

"Another one?" I ask. "Henry Jack already gave me the greatest."

I'm still holding the book, sometimes sniffing it, sometimes hugging it. My fingers keep stroking the pages, rubbing the cover.

"So," says Grandma, "are you ready for my surprise?" Her eyes shimmy with excitement.

"Yep," I say, remembering how I used to like a life with no surprises. But that was before Gibtown, before Florida, before the elephants and my mother and Henry Jack and trapeze flying. Before Boldo the Lion and George and Faith.

"You are going to freak out," says Trullia. She grins big with all her teeth showing.

"Soooooooooo," Grandma says, dragging out the suspense, "Trullia and I are making some major changes. I've decided to retire, to stop traveling with the circus. Trullia will still perform, and teach trapeze with Faith, but when we have time to relax at home . . ."

She pauses.

"Yes . . . ?" I say. "The suspense is killing me here."

"We'll have a second home, and it will be near you!" Grandma says. "I've decided to move my home base from Gibtown to Magic Mountain. I'm renting a cabin at the campground! Your dad got me a special deal. Life is too short to be so far away from the ones you love. Queenie Grace and her baby helped to teach me that."

"Sweet!" I say. "But . . . what about the elephants? You need to see them, too."

"Oh, I will," Grandma says. "That's why we're keeping this trailer in Gibtown. We'll split our time fifty-fifty: Florida and West Virginia. What your mother makes teaching trapeze with Faith will easily cover the lot rent for the trailer. And we'll all get to see one another a lot, like family is supposed to do."

"But . . . what about me?" asks Henry Jack. He tosses back his hair. "No fair," he says. "I always wanted to see snow, you know. Plus that blue-bottomed swimming pool at Magic Mountain, and the pirate-themed mini-golf, and the hiking trails . . ."

"Of course you'll visit West Virginia to see us," Grandma replies. "Don't worry, Henry Jack, you're like part of our family, too. We'll make sure to see you."

Henry Jack shrugs. I think his brow is furrowed, but you can never really tell, what with all the wrinkled skin.

"Okay," he says. "I guess. If you promise."

"So what do you think, Lily-Bird?" Grandma asks. "Family should be close, right?"

I nod.

"And I've decided to work less," Trullia says. "See you more. That's what's important. Flying is exciting and being famous is nice, but it's family that really matters. You'll be all grown up before we know it, and I don't want to miss so much from now on. My New Year's resolution is to spend more time . . . more time with you. I can't get back all that I lost, but I can start over brand-new."

I'm sitting next to Trullia on the sofa and she reaches over. Trullia makes the first move, and we squeeze each other tight. I feel her heart beating next to mine, hear her breath in my ear.

"I love you," Trullia says quietly. Her voice quivers; she's nervous.

I take a breath, draw it deep and far into my body, where I always kept all the feelings inside. From now on, I'm going to let them out, set them free.

"Love you, too," I say. The words feel good in my mouth, comfortable, as if I've been saying them all my life.

I'm so happy I could float away. I might not even need an airplane to get home.

"Lily Pruitt," says my mother, "you are one amazing girl."

"And now," Grandma states, "it's time for one more surprise!"

The door flies open, and Dad leaps into the room, spreading his arms wide.

"SURPRISE!" he yells.

I draw back; my eyes widen. I'm laughing and crying all at the same time.

"What—how? When—how did you get here? Why are you here?"

"He was worried sick about you having that asthma attack," Trullia says, "plus he was dying to meet Queenie Grace's baby. *Plus*, he wanted to come visit Grandpa's grave, and to give Grandma a hug. Said he was sadder and lonelier than he imagined with you gone. And so I pitched in on his airline ticket . . . and here he is!"

"I brought Christmas to you," Dad says. "So we'll be here for two more days. You'll only have to miss one day of school. Your school said it was cool because the trip is considered to be educational. And so is being with your family, both human and otherwise."

I'm dumbfounded, in shock. I stare at Trullia.

"You . . . did this for me? For *us*?" I ask.

She nods, smiles.

"Thanks so much," I say. "Thank you."

And then I whisper one word, under my breath, just for me: "Mom."

Her eyes fly wide; her eyebrows arch up. She says nothing, but I can tell that she heard that one word. Maybe one day, I'll say it out loud. She's one step closer to being a mom, a real mom like I always wanted.

"Thank you from me, too, Trullia," Dad says. "I'm happy to be here, and I know that Bill would be proud of you."

My parents exchange a glance, and I can actually see that maybe they really did love each other, once upon a time.

Dad looks away first and smiles at me.

"And because I brought Christmas to you, Lily, of course I had to bring this."

Dad unzips his suitcase, reaches in. He brings out the old golden star, our special Christmas tree star, the one that Grandpa and Grandma gave us so long ago.

"Put it on the tree," Grandma Violet says. "We need some light in this place."

Dad arranges the star just right, on the tip of the highest branch of Grandma's bare plastic green tree. He plugs it into an outlet on the wood-paneled wall. The star comes to life, shining a strong white light into Grandma's little trailer.

"There," Dad says, "it's lighting our way through another winter, and it'll be summer again before we know it."

Queenie Grace Likes Happily Ever After

I love it here: our wonderful new home at the sanctuary. All the green, the trees! It is so big . . . big like me. Big like my baby, Little Gray.

I look up at night, and I see Bill the Giant in the sky. I hear his voice. And I rejoice, to know that he is still here. People never really leave, and neither do elephants.

There's a kind lady who works here, an old lady with a minty smell. She has yellow hair and fancy cat's-eye glasses, and her cheeks are rosy with blush. Her name is Donna, and she knows exactly what we elephants are thinking, how we are feeling. Donna reads our minds, just takes a quiet peek inside the mysterious brains of Queenie Grace and Little Gray.

And today, Donna is here. So is Lily, and Lily's kind father, and Violet, and Trullia. Henry Jack, too. They are all here, a ring of family, a circle of happy.

Queenie Grace now loves Lily's father, too. There is always the chance to love someone new.

Donna peers quietly into my eyes, and I feel our connection: stretching back and forth. She looks into the eyes of my baby Little Gray. Her eyes shine behind her glasses.

"What the elephants want to say," Miss Donna announces to the humans, "is that they are very happy. They love this place, and they are thrilled that they can still paint. They say, 'That's not work, it's fun!' They are grateful to retire together, and to feel such a huge love for their young *mahout* Lily Pruitt."

Lily stretches both arms wide, to touch both me and Little Gray at the same time. She reaches so hard it's like she's trying to hug the earth, this whole big mysterious world full of surprises.

"I love both of you," Lily says to us. "And I think we need to give Baby more of a name."

Donna smiles. She knows Little Gray's name, because she sees it in my heart and mind.

"What are you thinking would be a good name for the baby?" Donna asks Lily.

Lily looks at my child. She squints, thinking. I concentrate, sending brain waves of the name into Lily's heart and mind.

"Well, she was once littler than Queenie Grace, and she's gray," Lily announces. "Let's call her 'Little Gray'! I don't even know where that name came from. It just popped into my head from out of nowhere."

"It's perfect," says Donna with a knowing smile. "Just perfect."

Donna and I exchange a glance. Little Gray and I each wrap a trunk around Lily's shoulders and hold her close. We will always watch over her, keep her safe. That is what Bill expects, and I like to please my best friend. My best *friends*.

"You know how they say an elephant never forgets?" Lily says. "It's more like a girl never forgets an elephant, once they've met and gotten to know each other."

"You should write a new *Manual for Mahouts*," says Henry Jack. "And put that in the book."

"The elephants agree that you should write a book," announces Donna. "And they say thank you, Lily. Thank you for saving them."

"Thank *you*," Lily says to my baby and me. "You sure did save me, too."

Oh, I know: This much is true. Because, you see, we elephants know more than most people believe.

Author's Note

I have always had a fascination and love for elephants, and knew that one day I'd write a book about an elephant. That day came when I heard Queenie Grace's voice in my mind, saying, *Bill the Giant has died and I cry. Elephants do cry.*

Queenie Grace came alive, and then Lily and the others followed. In researching the book, I found that many elephants live sad existences in captivity. I wanted to write about one who was loved . . . and then set free.

The first elephant brought to America traveled on a ship from India to New York in December 1796. Almost one hundred years later, an elephant named John L. Sullivan— "Old John"—performed a boxing act with his trainer, wearing a boxing glove on the end of his trunk. When he retired, Old John stayed on with the circus, babysitting the performers' children and leading the elephant herd to and from the show grounds and the trains.

There have been several famous circus elephants in America, including Jumbo, who was known as the biggest elephant in captivity. He debuted at Madison Square Garden in New York City on Easter Sunday, 1882.

Some elephants have died in strange and sad ways. One such elephant was Topsy, an attraction at a circus in Coney Island, New York. Topsy had at least three abusive trainers, including the last one, who tried to feed her a lit cigarette.

Not all elephant handlers and trainers are abusive. Many love their elephants and treat them as part of the family. My fictional Queenie Grace was lucky enough to have a trainer she loved, Bill the Giant.

There has been a lot of controversy about whether or not elephants should work in circuses or live in captivity. It is now estimated that twelve to fifteen thousand of the world's elephants are living in captivity.

Many circuses are now moving away from owning elephants. Feld Entertainment, parent company of Barnum & Bailey Circus and Ringling Brothers, retired their traveling elephants to Florida in 2016.

Some circuses and zoos are accused of mistreating elephants, confining them to tiny spaces and isolating them. Elephants are very social creatures in the wild, and they live in large, supportive family groups. Scientists say that elephants are the only animal to mourn their dead.

Some elephants don't seem to enjoy being showcased in circuses and zoos. Sanctuaries are being established to care for retired and displaced elephants, with the largest in America being the Elephant Sanctuary in Tennessee. The Elephant Sanctuary provides elephants with a natural habitat and individualized care. The habitat in which the elephants roam is not open to the public.

The Room to Roam sanctuary in this story is a fictional place, but many real ones exist throughout the world. To help elephants and to learn more, visit the websites below. Each and every elephant is One Amazing Elephant, and they all deserve to live with love and care.

www.elephantleague.org

www.elephants.com

www.elephantsanctuary.org

www.sheldrickwildlifetrust.org
(You can foster an orphaned baby elephant!)

www.pawsweb.org

www.elephantnaturepark.org

www.desertelephant.org

Acknowledgments

Thank you to:

PEN America and Phyllis Reynolds Naylor, for awarding the 2014 Working Writer Fellowship to my elephant and her tears.

My family of the heart at Vermont College of Fine Arts.

Super-Agent Rosemary Stimola, for loving Queenie Grace.

Wonder-Editors Annie Berger, Rosemary Brosnan, Jessica MacLeish, and all at HarperCollins.

The Fan Brothers—Eric and Terry—for the wonderful cover art.

The Highlights Foundation and Kent Brown.

John High, for building me the Writing Barn in which much of this book was written.

Marty Crisp, whose endless friendship in both good times and bad sustains me and my writing.

Annette Haas, my dad's angel, who made gentle caregiving an act of great love.

My family, both biological and not, and all the grandkiddos I love.

Angelina Cortez, for helping to create the bad guy with smoke and spurs (and her little sister Arianah, who cheered us on in antagonist-writing).

Harper Blaine, who came into our lives at just the right time: a godsend from above to make us smile during the most heartbreaking of days.

Zach High, for teaching me about unconditional love, determined hope, and unrelenting faith.

Connor and Justin Oatman, for making my heart grow twenty sizes larger the day I became M'Mere.